The Urbana Free Library

To renew: call 217-367-4057
or go to *urbanafreelibrary.org*
and select "My Account"

KISS ME
IN PARIS

KISS ME
IN PARIS

~ BY ~

CATHERINE RIDER

KCP Loft is an imprint of Kids Can Press

Text © 2018 Working Partners Ltd.
Series created by Working Partners Ltd.

Kids Can Press gratefully acknowledges the financial support of the Government
of Ontario, through the Ontario Media Development Corporation
for our publishing activity.

Published in Canada and the U.S. by Kids Can Press Ltd.
25 Dockside Drive, Toronto, ON M5A 0B5

Kids Can Press is a Corus Entertainment Inc. company

www.kidscanpress.com
www.kcploft.com

The text is set in Minion Pro and Claire Hand.

Edited by Kate Egan
Designed by Emma Dolan

Printed and bound in Altona, Manitoba, Canada in 6/2018 by Friesens Corp.

CM 18 0 9 8 7 6 5 4 3 2 1
CM PA 18 0 9 8 7 6 5 4 3 2 1

Library and Archives Canada Cataloguing in Publication

Rider, Catherine (Novelist), author
Kiss me in Paris / Catherine Rider.

ISBN 978-1-77138-867-2 (hardcover)
ISBN 978-1-5253-0142-1 (softcover)

I. Title.

PZ7.1 R53Kpa 2018   j813'.6   C2017-907149-1

To Lila, who I will never be able to thank enough

~ CHAPTER ONE ~

SERENA

FRIDAY, DECEMBER 21, 9:15 A.M.

This has to be what being dead feels like!

Even though I managed to sleep a little on my red-eye flight from New York, I'm still jet-lagged enough that my body feels far away. The street (or *rue*) in Paris's 7th arrondissement, where my big sister, Lara, is staying, looks like a faded photocopy of itself. But that might just be the December fog, which is so thick I didn't see *any* of the sights that Google Maps said my taxi was driving past — not even the Eiffel Tower!

I stumble out of the taxi and try not to face-plant on the sidewalk. Wouldn't *that* be a perfectly pathetic start to this trip — a two-day family adventure I dubbed "the Romance Tour." Some tour! Mom had to bail at the last minute, and Lara ignored all my "Can you pick me up from the airport?" emails, so right now, this is beginning to feel like the exact *opposite* of a "family trip."

I look left and right (my stiff neck screaming at me not to move so fast), scoping out as much of the street as the fog will allow. A cobblestoned road crawls away. The black awning of a café sits on top of the fog like a mud stain.

Maybe I shouldn't have spent so much time doing Google Image searches of Paris in the run-up to coming here. Everything looked so perfect on my laptop screen back home — all golden-hued street scenes and cafés dripping with flowers — that I'm starting to feel a little irked about how the real Paris looks: cold, dark and angry, just like any other city.

Then I look at the apartment building. The vintage brickwork and the way the wrought-iron balconies disappear into the fog makes everything feel so … *foreign*. In this moment, I feel every one of the 3,624 miles Google told me there were between here and home. I kind of wish I was in familiar old Brooklyn right now and not on some strange street in some strange city wondering why I'm looking at a *black* front door with a silver wreath, when Lara had told me the door would be red with a holly berry wreath. *Please* don't tell me that I somehow managed to direct the taxi to the wrong address. I can't even check my phone (*of course* I paid for a data roaming add-on), because it's in the left side pocket of my parka, which is currently barricaded by the tote bag that's hooked over my left shoulder. I'd have to set my bag down to free my arm — and honestly, I'm way too exhausted for that to be worth it.

Great idea to come in on a red-eye, Serena.

At least I'm in the right arrondissement, which is the fancy French word for Parisian neighborhood. The 7th might be one of the fanciest, because my guidebooks tell me that the Eiffel Tower is in this neighborhood, and so is the Musée d'Orsay, a few other Musées and the resting place of Napoleon. It would normally have been *way* beyond my accommodation budget for the Romance Tour, thanks to being centrally located on the Left Bank of the Seine River, but Lara *au pairs* for a family here in the city. A part of me is a little envious of how she found a part-time job she can easily fit around her studies, in *Paris*. But this is also the first time in history Lara has actually made something *easier* so … can't complain.

There is a flight of six stone steps up from the sidewalk, and I'm not only lugging my tote bag but a suitcase that weighs exactly fifty pounds (I know because I weighed it at home, on the scales in both my bathroom and Mom's, before I set off for JFK, maxing out the airline's allowance for checked luggage). After an eight-hour red-eye, these fifty pounds feel more like two hundred, and these six steps might as well be Mount Everest.

Get a hold of yourself, Fuentes, I think, trying to give myself a pep talk. *You've run half marathons! You can carry these fifty pounds up a few more steps.*

Besides … remember why you're here.

I shake out my hands, trying to de-cramp them. Then I hold my tote bag tighter to my ribs, grab the handle of my suitcase, grit my teeth and give a grunt that I am too tired to be embarrassed about — not that there's anyone on this *rue* to hear it.

At the top of Everest, I push the buzzer for Apartment 15. The voice on the intercom is crackly and speaking a rapid French that I don't understand at all, but it's still a voice I'd know anywhere.

"Lara, it's me," I tell my sister.

"*Serena?*" I wonder if she's just woken up because she sounds surprised. *She didn't seriously forget about the Romance Tour, did she?*

Lara tells me to come to the fourth floor. *Awesome.* I drag my exactly-fifty-pound suitcase up the stairs — because *of course* there's no elevator, and *of course* Lara hasn't thought to come and help me — and I look at the numbers on the apartments on the fourth floor: *10, 11, 12 ...* There are three apartments on each floor, so Apartment 15 is *not* here. I have to schlep up *another* flight of stairs, because I've just remembered the ground floor isn't considered the first floor over here.

Why? Whyyyyyy, Europeans?

"So, wha ... What are you doing here?" Lara's standing in the doorway of Apartment 15, waiting for me. I'd have been relieved to see her if she didn't look so completely confused. She's in sweats, and her hair (she got the lustrous waves, while I got the wild, frizzy curls) is kind of all over the place, supporting my just-woke-up theory. She's still got her signature bright-red lipstick on, though. I'm not sure I've seen her without it since she started high school.

I ignore her for a moment, heaving my suitcase into the apartment, straight into a bright and spacious living room, where I prop it against a couch. "Give me a minute," I tell her. Then I point to one of the doors leading off the living room. "Bathroom?"

"Yeah," she says, looking like she thinks this is a weird dream she's going to wake up from any second.

When I come back from the bathroom, I walk by her and

collapse onto the tan couch. It's so soft and squishy I nearly bounce off. I notice a small Christmas tree in a corner. It's decorated with black-and-gold bows. So chic, so *French*. I get myself together and give Lara my best glare. "Soooo … what happened this morning? You forgot to check your phone for an email from your sister? You forgot about our plan to see all the sights our parents saw on their honeymoon? You forgot about the *Romance Tour*?"

"I didn't *forget* …" She sits on the arm of the couch, looking at me like *I'm* the flaky one. "But you know … once Mom got called away on that conference, I kind of assumed we'd be calling off the whole Paris thing, and that you and I would fly separately to London to meet Mom on Christmas Eve."

Jet lag has not only made my eyes go a little weird, it seems to be scrambling my brain. Because that's the only reason I could be imagining my sister forgetting about our *carefully thought-out* plans to travel through Paris, seeing all the places our parents did when they honeymooned here almost exactly twenty-five years ago. I spent a weekend's worth of hours — time I could've spent studying for finals, which, believe me, are no joke at Columbia — coming up with our itinerary. I'd emailed it to Lara and asked for her thoughts. Not that I ever heard anything back.

Oh, God. It's all making a terrible kind of sense.

I stare at her, hoping to win her back with facts. "Counterpoint. I told you I was still coming to Paris."

"You did? When?"

I sit up, as much as I can — it's not easy. The couch is trying to swallow me, and I'm tired enough to let it. "In *every email* I've sent you this week. I said, three times, 'Can't wait to *see you* in Paris, sis!' I told you the flight number, my arrival time ... I told you how much money to set aside for food and Metro fares. Literally the only thing you had to take care of was meeting me at the airport!"

"I thought the tour was called off," she says weakly. "I ... I've been really busy. I haven't been checking email that often."

Meaning you haven't been reading my *emails.* "Just because Mom can't make it, that doesn't mean *we* can't do the tour and put together a scrapbook to give her on New Year's Day" — I'm telling her this even though I've said exactly these things in all the emails she obviously *didn't read* — "while we're all together in London, for their twenty-fifth anniversary. You know New Year's Day has been hard for Mom since ..."

I don't finish that sentence. I can't.

Then my sister gives me what the family calls the Lara Look — wide-eyed, her expression frozen like her brain's a computer that has eighty-four tabs open, all of them trying to download something and a couple of them troubled by adware. It's the look she always gives when she *knows* she's screwed up. She mumbles something about being really sorry. "I thought you were emailing to remind me to get Mom a Christmas gift."

"Did you even do *that*?" The words are out before I can stop them. I know Lara well enough to know that when she's giving the Look, she's also beating herself up. I shouldn't make it worse, but I can't help it this morning — I've traveled 3,624 miles with a suitcase that weighs one-third of me!

"I was going to pick something up in Madrid."

I pinch the bridge of my nose, feeling a stress headache coming on. "Madrid? What are you talking about? Madrid has *never* been a stop on the tour!"

A sheepish look crosses her face. "Well, I … wasn't talking about you and me."

It's only now that I notice her red lipstick is slightly smeared, in addition to the messy hair, only now that my nose twitches at the scent of cologne that has been present this whole time.

Lara has *company.*

I look around, like he might be standing perfectly still in a corner or something, but he must be hiding in another room. If only I knew the French for "Come out, come out, wherever you are!"

Then I notice … *other suitcases.* None as big as mine, but there are three of them, surrounding the fancy coffee table in the middle of the room.

"What's going on?"

Lara tucks her hair behind her ears, then crosses her arms over her chest. Looks at the floor. "Damn it, this is a total disaster."

"You're seriously going to Madrid? What are you going to Madrid for?"

Then, the reason Lara has been too busy to read any of my emails comes strolling out of one of the doors. He's a tall dude who is (of course) model handsome even while wearing a jersey of what I figure is some French soccer team. High cheekbones, sun-kissed skin, dark wavy hair that's a bit long but somehow perfectly swept back. He smiles at me, then mumbles something to Lara, in French. She mumbles back, *"Tout va bien,"* a couple times.

Then the guy looks at me and moves forward, holding out his hand and nodding. *"Bonjour."*

I accept his handshake, hoping he's not going to try to pull me in for a double-cheek kiss, because I suck at those even when I'm well rested. (*Right cheek first? Left cheek first? Oh, sorry, we totally misread each other and now my nose is in your mouth.*) I'm so annoyed with Lara, I don't say *"Bonjour"* back to him — I say, "Hey, what's up?" in the broadest, flattest-A, most *American* accent that I can manage. I actually get a bit of a Southern twang in there, even though I've never been south of Philadelphia at any point in my life.

One corner of his mouth rises in a half-smile, and I can't tell if it's a smug smirk or not. "We 'av confusion, *oui?*"

Lara's still looking at the carpet. "Serena, this is Henri. Henri, this is my little sister, Serena. She just got in from New York."

Henri smiles the second half of his smile — okay, he's not smug — then nods as he looks back to Lara. He says something in French; Lara replies in French. Henri says something else in French, and I wonder if it's all right for me to go in the kitchen and make myself a cup of coffee, but I can't do that because I'm slowly sinking back down into the couch. So tired. Henri's rubbing Lara's arm in what looks like a reassuring way. I can see from the soft, tender look in his eyes that this dude is super-into my sister, and I wonder — not for the first time — how she copes with her studies and her job if every week she's falling in love with a new guy.

Then I tell myself not to be bitter about people being in love, just because I've never even been in serious *like*.

"Hey," I interrupt all the French. Sit up straight. "Real life — no subtitles. What's going on?"

Lara looks at me, half-throwing up her hands, then running

them through her hair again. "Since Henri and I won't be seeing each other for almost a month, when classes start up again, he bought tickets for us to go to Madrid for a couple of days, before flying to meet you and Mom in London."

Wow. Lara's going on a trip with a guy? She *never* does anything like that. It's way too much commitment.

Henri makes a show of giving a shrug that's more gallant than Gallic. "Zis is your sist*err*. We can go to Madrid in Januar*ee*. It will still be there, *non*? Eets okay, *tout va bien*."

Lara's got a pained look on her face, and I can tell that this scheduling conflict is not an accident. She's always wanted to go to Madrid — and, now that I think about it, she hasn't been all *that* enthusiastic about the Romance Tour. Maybe because it involves talking about Dad, and Lara *never* brings him up.

My sister might be scatterbrained sometimes, but now I'm wondering — have *I* been oblivious?

"No, you know what?" I say, making a snap decision. This whole tour was *my* idea. The scrapbook will be a nice gift for Mom, but there's something else I want from this trip. And maybe I can only get it if I do this by myself. "You guys should go."

"Are you sure?" Lara is still looking pained, and I'm kind of glad that she feels bad for leaving, even though it's obvious she'd rather be in Madrid.

"I'm sure. Just make sure you get Mom a *great* gift!"

Lara hugs me — grateful *and* relieved, I can tell. "Thank you, Serena. You're the best!"

She doesn't have to tell *me* that. "Shut up — no, I'm not. And anyway, at least I can get some sleep — I'll crash in your room."

The Lara Look is back. "Ugh. The thing is, the family I work for has gone to Zurich for Christmas, and this apartment is being deep-cleaned while they're gone. I promised them the place would be empty when the cleaners arrived — which is today."

As I sigh and briefly look up to the ceiling, she reaches out to me. "It's only one night, though — maybe you could get a hotel?"

Numbers fly through my mind, as I try to make a Paris hotel room fit my budget, not to mention my plan. I would need one hour — at least — to find a hotel, then thirty to forty-five minutes, probably, to get to said hotel and drop off my luggage, and at least ninety euros (but probably more if I want clean sheets and no bedbugs) to pay for it all ...

"I'm not sure I can afford it."

Lara turns back to Henri, apologetic. "Maybe I should stay ... I can't leave my little sister alone in a strange city."

But Henri is smiling and taking a cell phone from his back pocket. "Eets no problem*m*. I 'av idea." Then he dials and has a super-fast, very French conversation with someone. In less than two minutes, *voilà* (his word, not mine):

"Eets okay. You sleep with our friend, Jean-Luc."

I stare at him. "I'm sorry, *what?*"

But Lara has her hands over her face, and her shoulders are shaking from laughing. "That's not what he means! He means, you can stay in Jean-Luc's dorm. His roommate is away for the holidays, so you'll have your own bedroom, all to yourself. It'll be great."

"Um ... but I'll be staying with some strange French guy! No offense, Henri."

Henri grins at us both, although he looks as lost among our rapid English as I feel during all the French.

"Jean-Luc *is* a little strange," Lara says. "But he's actually really nice, once you get to know him." That last part she says under her breath. I don't know how much time she expects me to spend with him. I have an itinerary planned, after all, so I probably won't say more than a few words to this "Jean-Luc" character.

"Also," Lara goes on, "he's half-American, so he speaks English really well. You'll get along just fine. Here" — she writes something on a map of the Paris transit system, which she then hands to me — "this should help you get around."

I take it and hope my face doesn't show my disbelief that my own sister doesn't know me well enough to know that I came here with three maps of the Metro.

"I've written Jean-Luc's number at the top."

I enter the number into my phone, realizing that I've "agreed" to crash with some half-American boy who is really nice but also strange. It's not ideal, but I don't see any other choice right now. "Fine," I say, with a shrug. "I probably won't see him much, anyway."

Lara's looking at me again — confused, like before, but also a little wary and concerned. "You're really going to walk around Paris all by yourself?"

For a second, I have to look away, because Lara's eyes narrow in the exact way that our dad's used to whenever *he* was concerned about me. Whenever I would pretend to him I wasn't upset about something. I look back at her, hoping my voice doesn't rat me out by cracking.

"I am. I have to."

Lara steps forward and pulls me into a big hug — only the second one she's given me since I got here, nearly five minutes ago, which is way below her batting average. She pulls away from me, holding my hands and staring at me. There are tears in her eyes.

"Mayonnaise?" she asks me. When we were little, we both hated mayonnaise and would vow to eat a jar of it if we ever broke a promise. Even though we are both older, and both kind of like mayo now, it's still our sisterly code for *Trust me*.

I nod, because I know if I try to speak, my voice *will* rat me out.

Henri clears his throat and says something in French. Lara responds in English: "I know, I know." Then, to me: "We have to go soon if we're going to make our train."

I nod again and dare to speak: "I understand." Another hug, and then I pick up my exactly-fifty-pound suitcase and haul it out of the apartment.

When I'm at the top of the stairs, Lara's voice drifts toward me.

"Hey, sis, maybe you should let Henri carry that down for you."

I'm halfway through insisting that I've got it, when my muscles give out, my hand cramps and I watch fifty pounds of luggage tumble down the flight of stairs.

CHAPTER TWO

JEAN-LUC

9H45

Why did I answer my phone?

I've been ignoring it for the last three weeks, ever since Martine decided that, rather than merely break up, she'd prefer to live in our breakup conversation forever, but today, I actually looked to see who was calling me, in case it wasn't her, and *now* ...

Now, Henri has roped me into babysitting Lara's little sister, because I was the idiot who told him that Olivier would be driving to Lille on some emotional suicide mission to win back his *lycée* girlfriend. Which means there is a spare room at our dorm. Which means I am now taking down all my photographs and clearing out all my notes and equipment from my temporary studio, so this stranded American girl has somewhere to sleep tonight.

Well, I will give her the spare room and the spare key, but I cannot do more than that. I have a project to finish for when classes start up again in January — and three weeks ago, I had to start *all over again*, because I realized that my very giving ex-girlfriend had so distracted me, I was producing poorly framed, amateurish work. I hope that this American girl doesn't expect me to play tour guide, because I really can't handle that right now. I mean, of course, I'll make sure I'm contactable in case she gets into some sort of trouble. But I can't literally watch her all day.

I'm trying to arrange my photos in a neat pile without looking too closely at them. They only make me wince, especially the shots of rue Lamarck, in Montmartre, at dawn. For some reason, I got it into my head that what those shots needed was to be at a ninety-degree angle. I may have been going for something with that, but I'll be damned if I can remember what it was. Usually, when I look at my photos, I know exactly what I was trying to achieve — even when I don't really meet my own goals. But this time, I cannot remember anything except crouching down and turning the camera over in my hands, as if that was going to magically make things more interesting. It did not.

The corner of my sleeve brushes the pile and several photos cascade to the floor. I'm tempted to yell all the swear words I know in two languages as I pick them up again.

But I don't do this. I take a deep breath and ask myself, is it really the prospect of a houseguest that has me in this mood? Am I sure it wasn't the red badge? The red badge in the bottom-right corner of my cell phone screen that tells me I received a voice mail from PAUL THAYER at 6h05.

Paul Thayer is my father. He lives in New Jersey, so he was

technically calling me a little after midnight, his time, but I would not be surprised if he was confused and somehow thought that Paris was six hours *behind* the East Coast. Either that, or he actually expected me to be up that early. If he knew *anything* about me, he'd know that I've never been a morning person.

I haven't listened to the voice mail. I don't even need to. I know it will be a variation on the voice mail I got from him *last* Christmas:

Son, I'm so sorry I can't get to Paris this December like I usually do. (He says that like him visiting is an annual tradition, even though he's skipped the last seven years.) *But I can make it up to you. Julie and I would really love it if you could make it out to Jersey this summer. You know we'll take great care of you, although I understand you might, uh ... you know, have to* stay *in Paris for the summer.*

The man has not visited me for seven Christmases and seven birthdays but expects me to travel to another continent by myself, to hang out with him and his second family? That we will have things to talk about, bond over? That I'll suddenly connect with his twin sons, whom I haven't seen since he brought them to Paris as screaming toddlers?

I walk out of Olivier's room and into mine. I place my portfolio (the zombie of my project) on top of my laptop and try not to pay attention to how messy and cluttered my desk is. Try not to think — again — about how a photo of Montmartre is always going to be a photo of Montmartre, whether the camera has been turned ninety degrees or not. Try not to think any more about how I am producing uninspired work for this project. Try not to dread how Monsieur Deschamps, my advisor, is going to give me another one of his lectures. A portfolio of simple shots of Paris, he will say, does not meet the assignment's objective of "telling a story from the city."

"Where are the people?" he asked me on Wednesday, when I popped into his office for an end-of-term consultation. I told him, the people were there — surely, every piece of art contains pieces of the artist?

He told me to "stop being such a pretentious young fool. Connect with your subject. Remember, you're trying to capture a city. A city's heart is not just its streets, its sights — it is in its people."

I chose not to inform him that, having recently broken up with my girlfriend and said goodbye to my dormmates — who all went home for Christmas — I am somewhat short on people right now. And photographing people has never been one of my strengths. Some of my classmates seem to just *know* the right moment to capture a smile. A pensive look or a flash of wonder. But that involves spending time with the subject, keeping them loose, engaged. And then getting them to stand still long enough for you to get a good shot.

Convincing people to stand still has never come naturally to me. And now, four days before Christmas, I have the whole dorm to myself, so there's no one in here for me to even *ask* to stand still. Well, there's this American girl who's due any minute now, but I can hardly ask her, can I? Henri said she had a list of things she *really* wanted to do while she was here. I might be able to venture outside and get some shots of strangers instead. Though I've barely been able to see more than a dozen meters out my window, because of a thick fog that does not seem to want to lift.

Reception buzzes me, and I go downstairs to the lobby. As stressed and irritated as I am, I still can't stop my brain from noting all the details, in case there's something new to capture. The lobby is kind of drab, with an ancient, artificial Christmas tree in one corner looking like a smudge of moss against the dull brick walls — a weak effort to give the place some "seasonal cheer." A Latina girl is standing by the front desk, where Thierry the concierge is not even pretending to look up from his copy of *L'Équipe*. In front of her is a bulging suitcase, with a tote bag on top — a traveler with a lot to do while she's here. She's about the same height as me. Her long, slightly frizzy black hair is tied back, and she's not wearing makeup. She has a knee-length, black down parka over dark blue jeans and a purple sweater. Black boots. It's only as I look at her that I realize I was not expecting this inconvenient guest to look both very American *and* naturally stylish. I raise a hand to signal that I'm the guy she's looking for, and she starts to say something that *might* be French.

Then again, it could also be Swahili.

"It's okay," I tell her. "I speak English. You are Serena?"

"That's right."

"I am Jean-Luc." I reach out to shake her hand, but when she takes mine, she leans forward, turning her face away, offering her cheek. I don't expect this from an American girl, so I do nothing — I stand still, holding her hand, until she turns her face to look at me, extracting her hand from mine as if we didn't just have an awkward non-kiss.

Through a weary smile, she thanks me for taking her in.

"It's okay," I say again. "You must be kind of tired. Henri said you were on an overnight flight and arrived less than an hour ago."

"Yep, that's me. Direct from New York."

"Let me carry your luggage." I gesture that she should go upstairs.

"Thank you." She hooks her tote bag over one shoulder, then walks past me.

Once Serena is halfway up the stairs, Thierry looks up from his newspaper. Gives me a suspicious look. In French, I tell him: "She's my friend from America."

I bend down to pick up Serena's suitcase and almost dislocate my shoulder.

The thing feels like it weighs twenty kilos!

✳

Serena is in the living room sitting on the chaise longue, her head leaning back. She's certainly made herself at home.

"I really hope I'm not putting you out," she tells me. Like most Americans I've encountered in Paris, her voice is so *loud* — like she is yelling at someone, except she is not. It seems to rattle the walls of my dorm.

"It is no problem," I tell her, dragging the suitcase to the spare room. I keep my body and head turned from her as I wipe the sweat from my brow. "This is where you can sleep. I imagine you will want to rest after your flight, *non*?"

She sits straight up, like a vampire in an old-time Hollywood movie. Swings her legs off the chaise longue. "Can't. I have a plan! Besides, I made sure to research the best travel pillows, so I slept a little during the flight. And even if I didn't, I'd still have to get going, because I'm already running behind. I've got so much to see. The Louvre, the Seine, the Eiffel Tower. I need to get started!"

I wonder if she has decided to fight jet lag with coffee. Lots of coffee. So that she can stomp around the most popular sights of Paris. The ones everybody ticks off, like the city is a to-do list.

But then a thought strikes me.

All these places are the most crowded … where better to find people for my project?

"Well, if you're sure you don't need to rest …" I lean down to gather up my camera, which I've been leaving on the coffee table now that Olivier isn't here to complain about "clutter." I hook the camera over my neck, letting it hang over my chest. "I have a little bit of work to do on my photography project" — *that's an understatement!* — "but I guess I could show you around Paris for a little while."

Serena is digging into the tote bag at her feet. "Oh, you don't have to do that. I have four maps, an almost fully charged phone and three guidebooks. I'll be fine."

She does have all these things. She shows them to me.

"You will not experience the soul of the city from just this book," I tell her. "You must not go only to museums and tourist sights. You must take the Metro, walk the streets, look at the architecture, listen to the sounds of the city. You must let it speak to you. *Then*, you will feel like you have really been here. If you let me, I can take you to many great places that the writers of this book never even heard of. *Real* Paris." I may not have captured it on film — yet. But I know it is there.

"Oh, I'm not here for 'real' Paris," she tells me, picking up one of the guidebooks.

"I do not understand."

She hesitates, but then her eyes soften and she speaks. "The thing is … I'm here for my parents. They came to Paris on their honeymoon, almost twenty-five years ago. Both of them always said it was the best, most magical trip they ever took together. And, for the last two years, my mom always gets very sad around Christmas and New Year, because she's reminded of … who's not here. I thought, if I could tour the city, see all the sights they did, put together a scrapbook for her to keep, it will remind her of happier times. Maybe she won't be as sad this time of year …"

Her voice catches, and she looks back down to the guidebook. Flicks through it, front to back, then back to front. I can tell she's not actually reading anything, just keeping herself occupied and letting the moment pass. I can see her struggling to keep emotions off her face.

The camera at my chest suddenly feels heavy. I reach for it and take her photo.

Her head snaps up, and she's scowling. In fairness, I might have earned the scowl — that was a really private moment I just stole from her. But the photo does look great.

"*Pardon.*" I look at the floor and try to will away the blood that rises into my cheeks. "I am studying photography. It is an 'abit."

Yes, I *am* making myself sound just a little bit more French to give myself more chance of being forgiven.

"That's okay," she says. I am about to ask her if she studies — and, if so, what — but she is pulling a smart faux leather cross-body bag out of the tote bag and stuffing her guidebooks and itinerary and maps into it. "I should get started. Is there a spare key I can borrow?"

This is a most curious turn of events — a few minutes ago, I was looking forward to shaking off this American girl, but now, as she's getting ready to leave, I want to follow her. She's my best hope of getting good shots for my project. It could even be ironic — pretentious crowd shots where the sea of humanity obscures one's view of the world's greatest city.

Actually, that's not a bad idea.

"Surely," I say, "you would prefer someone who *knows* the city to go with you? What if you get lost?"

"I'm an expert at Google Maps." But then she pauses, sighs, looks at me. Not withering or offended this time — more curious. "I guess if you want to tag along for a while, that'd be okay."

For some reason, when *she* says "tag along," I feel a bit embarrassed.

"But I warn you," she continues, "I have a lot of places to get to and not a lot of time to get to them, so I think I'm probably going to be moving too fast for you to take any good photos of stuff."

How does she have so much energy? I shrug, aware that I'm trying to make sure I don't shrug too "Frenchly."

"What is first?" I ask.

"The Louvre," she says, crossing the room to where I left her suitcase. She sets it down and unzips it. Removes a pair of bright orange sneakers that change my opinion of her sense of style. "And we need to get going, because the whole mix-up with Lara has cost me too much time."

She changes out of her boots into the hideous sneakers, then scoops up her cross-body bag and is out the door before I can even mentally list what lenses I should bring with me. I hear her voice over her footsteps as she heads back downstairs. I swear, I can hear her from the lobby!

"You coming or what?"

I can tell that this American girl, with the orange feet, is not going to slow down. And even though it feels *wrong* to venture out into the world with only a single lens on my camera — looking at the world with just one pair of eyes, *mon dieu!* — here I am running out the door after her, strangely eager to spend a day seeing a tourist's Paris.

Just how badly do I not want to be alone today?

CHAPTER THREE

SERENA

10:25 A.M.

"Hey," I call back to Jean-Luc, as I march along a bridge called Pont du Carrousel, on our way to the Louvre. "Why don't I just meet you back at the dorm?"

It shouldn't have taken us this long to get here, but ever since we got off the Metro at Palais Royal, we've been stalled by his constant need to fall back and take photos of whatever catches his eye. I know he's got a project to finish, but it's not like I'm ever going to see it, so I don't need to stand next to him while he takes shots of streetlamps or people lined up for a bus. I've got places to be! I appreciate that he's come this far, but it really does seem like it would be easier for both of us if we just went our separate ways right now. I guess he doesn't agree, though, because here he comes, expensive camera around his neck, mumbling an apology as he jogs to catch up as we come off the bridge, walking along Place du Carrousel toward the courtyard.

I'd like to say that I'm wowed by my first sight of the Louvre, but there's not much to see this morning — the whole place is shrouded by the fog encircling Paris like a giant claw. We cross the courtyard, to the great glass pyramid in the center. And of course, Jean-Luc stops again. Looks at me with that expression of his — lips pursed, the angles of his face looking sharp enough to draw blood, his eyes narrowed like everything he says is deep and meaningful. I think to myself that he couldn't look much more French if he had a neat goatee and was carrying a baguette. Then I wonder if it's okay that I'm thinking in such stereotypes.

But I'll bet he's thought of me as a "typical American" at some point already today.

"Serena …" That accent of his seems to get stuck every time it hits one of the vowels in my name. "You must stop. Look. See. This is the Pyramide du Louvre."

I don't stop, look or see. I rush across the stone courtyard with the confidence of someone who has been here many times — or someone who has watched and rewatched a bunch of virtual tours on YouTube. I join the line for those who have prebooked, standing behind a couple who sounds German, scarves pulled up over their faces to protect them from the windchill. Just like my guidebook predicted, this close to Christmas means the line is not all that long (directly opposite, on the other side of the pyramid, is a much longer line for the More Impulsive Tourists, without reservations — or, as I call them, Crazy People).

"I know all about the pyramid," I tell Jean-Luc, as he joins me in the line. "Designed by I. M. Pei, completed in 1989. Made up of

673 glass panes — *not* 666, as some people like to think. I've read everything I need to read."

He shakes his head at me. "You cannot absorb Paris from Wikipedia," he says.

"I'm not here to 'absorb' Paris," I tell him, as the line shuffles forward a few feet. I'm getting a weary sense of déjà vu — like I'm back at customs in the airport. Just, you know, with an icy cold wind whipping my face. It's annoying and kind of painful, but in a strange way it's almost nice to actually *feel* something. The floating sensation of jet lag — or maybe *something else* — had been starting to worry me. "I only have one day here, remember? So I have to be quick. There are six pieces of art that I have to see and get photos of for my scrapbook. Once I have them, I'm out of the Louvre and heading to the next spot."

I look over my shoulder and catch him peering at me, again — neither totally horrified nor outraged, just mildly contemptuous. It makes me feel oddly embarrassed, self-conscious — but it would take too long for me to explain to him that while I *do* appreciate art and culture, it's not my *priority* today. I'm here for a different reason. I raise my hands in a gesture that says, *Seriously, dude, you can take off anytime you like.* But he's not looking at me now — he's checking out the Crazy People line, obviously trying to calculate how long he's going to have to stand there to catch up with me.

He must really, really like the Louvre.

"I have an extra ticket," I tell him. In fact, I have two, because I prebooked for me, Mom and Lara) *weeks* ago. "You can take it, if you really want to go in."

"*Merci*," he says. "But … do you really mean to run from painting to painting?"

"If I have to, to keep to my schedule."

"How will you remember what you have seen, if you are always running?"

I say nothing. Think to myself: *I'm not here to remember for me.*

Jean-Luc is still talking. "You will not have an experience if you don't slow down."

I'm not so sure I agree with that. I'm here to walk in my parents' footsteps, to follow the trail they once took through the city, at a time when they were young and in love. I'm here to *understand* their experience, not have one of my own. So what if I do it a little fast?

Jean-Luc's *still* talking, but I've missed some of what he's saying: "… absorb the art, its meaning? How can it" — he clicks his fingers, I guess trying to find the words in English — "move you if *you* are the one who is moving?"

Pretty nice wordplay for a guy using his second language. Although, Lara said he's half-American, so I guess he probably grew up speaking both. "I'm not here to be moved," I say, as we finally walk through the pyramid doors, putting our bags through the security scanner. "I've got to see six things and hope that there aren't walls of people in the way, so I can get my photos. And then, I've got to move on to a bookstore called Shakespeare and Company, because there's something I want to find."

He peers at me again, looking pained. Or offended. Maybe both.

I'm really wishing he would leave.

I turn away from him as we take the escalators down to the atrium, to signal that my focus is now solely on the museum — getting in, getting my photos and getting out. I say what I should have said back at the dorm, or at any point between there and here. "You really don't *have* to join me."

What I don't say: *Why do you* want *to join me? My own mom and sister (who I wanted to do this trip for) both chose to skip it, so why are you so eager to tag along? You can take photos anywhere.*

And, like, seriously, Lara? You didn't think that your easily distracted photographer buddy might not *be the best person to pair up with your super-organized sister?*

Another *click* — probably the fortieth time I've heard it since we left the dorm. He's taken my picture again, not even trying to hide it at this point. I'm too agitated about keeping to my schedule to think much about whether this is okay.

He lets the camera hang down, looking at me intently. Then he shrugs and says, "Why not, ah? I have never actually seen the *Mona Lisa.*"

I try not to scoff. He was so outraged when I said I needed to get in and out of the Louvre — and he hasn't even *seen* one of the pieces of Great Art that's supposed to move me. How much "absorbing" does he do, if he's never laid eyes on the most famous painting in this entire museum? Maybe he's like the New York hipster I've met occasionally — usually, guys that Lara is loving and leaving — who are too busy Keeping It Real to ever actually go and visit the Statue of Liberty …

And they are very, very eager to tell you that.

I shrug at him again, trying not to think about how many times I've done that today, on what is supposed to be a great romantic tour through Paris. "Whatever," I tell him, as we reach the twin booths, handing over our tickets for inspection. "Just do me a favor and try to keep up, okay?"

*

When we pass the checkpoint, the first thing I notice is a tiny image of the *Mona Lisa*, pinned to a wall. It's black and white, on what looks like a sheet of loose-leaf paper that's been put through a typical printer — like the kind we'd use in high school or in the library at college — with an arrow that directs you to the painting itself. We follow these low-tech signs through the Louvre, and every other piece of art that we pass seems to recede into the walls, like, *Yeah, we know what you're here for. Go say hello to her, it's fine — we're not going anywhere. You can see us after.*

It doesn't take long to reach the right gallery, and we go inside, caught in the slipstream of the other rushing tourists. The room is vast, the ceiling is high and even though the conversations are muted, they echo loudly. This is not the peaceful experience I assumed it would be. The crowd is three-deep at the *Mona Lisa* when we get there, and I have to tiptoe to get a glimpse of her — which is hard, because, well, she's kind of tiny. I don't know why, but I expected her to be bigger than me. On the bare wall behind a glass case in a room that's as big as some of the lecture theaters back at Columbia, she seems so ... *small*. And the colors are all muted browns and blacks, so it's not like the painting pops and draws the eye, no matter where you stand.

I figure maybe she'll look more impressive when I'm up close. I keep my eyes lowered until I can get a good look, a *real* look — saving the experience for when I can really appreciate it.

It takes a few minutes to shuffle forward so that I'm close enough to get within range to take a photo for Mom's scrapbook. At first, I hold the phone up over my head, but no matter how many times I try, I can't avoid the hills of bobble hats, baseball caps and shawls between me and the painting. More than once, half the space in my photo is robbed by someone taking a selfie — someone grabbing some proof that they were *here*, in the Louvre.

I shuffle forward some more, trying to get to the front. I'm not one of those dainty girls whose nonexistent body weight allows them to magically move through crowds, and I also don't want to tread on anyone else's experience by asking them, "Hey, would you mind?," so this process takes longer than I would like. And when I finally do make it to the front, just a retractable belt between me and the Most Famous Piece of Art Ever, the first thing I notice is that it's impossible to get a decent photo, because no matter where I move my head, I can't escape the green glow from the exit sign on the opposite wall, reflected on the protective glass placed over the painting. It's so annoying, I half-expect Mona — or is it Lisa? — herself to throw up her hands and ask one of the guards, can they *do something* about this?

I have to crouch down and take the photo from underneath the belt. Then I stand up and put my phone away so that I can get a "good" look — experience the *Mona Lisa*, the beautiful lady with the facial expression nobody can agree on. Leonardo da Vinci's masterpiece.

I'm starting to think that I must be missing the point because, apparently, people come see this painting and have *reactions* to it or something. But I'm not having one at all. I feel like I'm missing whatever there is to *get* about this piece. Sure, it's nice and all, but it's just a portrait of some lady. She might be smiling, she might not be — I don't really get what difference it makes either way or why so many people seem to think it matters.

What has possessed all these people to endure being squashed together like tweens at a One Direction concert? I'm starting to feel a bit claustrophobic. I see Jean-Luc staring right at the painting, his expression as unreadable as Mona's. He seems to sense me looking at him, stares back at me for a moment, then looks down at his camera, as if he hadn't been totally transfixed. Whatever. I got my picture, so I can leave. I'm about to tell him this, when I realize that there's, like, eight people between us, and I really don't want to be the Loud American shouting over other tourists. So I just point to myself, then over the heads of the people arriving at the back of the group. *I'm moving on to the next piece.*

I don't need subtitles to understand his expression: *Already? Are you serious?*

I really don't have time to get into a mime-off with him, so I just tap the watch I'm not wearing, then shrug and smile apologetically in what I hope translates to: *Thank you so much for getting me here, have a good day, and I'll see you back at the dorm … maybe.*

Then I turn around and weave my way through the human tide. I have five more pieces to see, and then I can get out of here. If I run, I might just make it to Shakespeare and Company by a quarter after noon, which would be close enough to on schedule that my jaw might start unclenching.

"Serena ..." He's actually following me. I stop to let him catch up. "You are not impressed?" he asks.

"I'm not here to be impressed," I tell him. "I'm just here to get some photos."

"You are here just to be here." What, in an American accent, might sound no more meaningful than a line from a Coldplay song, in a slightly French accent, it sounds like the kind of Big Thought had only by, like, serious guys in the nineteenth century who wore monocles and had epic beards and smoked pipes as they hunched over parchment with quills. The way Jean-Luc says it, I feel like he's expecting me to respond, but — whether it's jet lag or the stress of being behind schedule — I don't have anything to say. I'm here on serious business, but not *that* kind of serious. I don't care if it makes me shallow in his eyes, I'm not doing this to experience art, not looking to expand my mind or grow or whatever he thinks might happen if I gawk at some painting long enough. I'm here for different reasons. So what if I'm trying to get through the Louvre in under an hour? The way Mom always tells it, she and Dad didn't spend all day here — I bet they actually saw everything they intended to see, because neither of them would stall repeatedly. Getting here was one of Dad's lifetime ambitions, but he was still the type of guy who would come here with a *plan*, one that he would *stick to*. Mom would have been the same —

they wouldn't stop just so they could bicker about whether or not the other was moved by something.

"Serena?" Jean-Luc's looking at me again — not offended now, just curious.

"I don't know why everyone goes crazy for that," I say, pointing back to the *Mona Lisa*, barely visible through a forest of selfie sticks. "I mean, look at this ..." I turn to the piece that is hanging on the wall directly opposite da Vinci's. It's a giant painting, and I mean *giant* — I've been in swimming pools that are smaller — depicting what I at first think is meant to be the Last Supper. But then I notice that there's a whole *party* going on all around Jesus and the Apostles, and I don't know if I remember *that* from the Bible. "Look at this. Or that —" I don't point at anything specific, just the numerous paintings that, now that I've seen the *Mona Lisa*, seem comfortable stepping forward and asking for attention. "There're things *happening* in these paintings. The *Mona Lisa* is just sitting there, smirking. Or maybe not, obviously, but still."

I notice that he's looking at me now. I can't read his face, but I don't *think* he's being haughty again, although his eyes *are* narrowed.

"Look," I say, "museums are not really my thing. You want someone to be moved by art, ask my sister if she wants to come here next semester. She gets this stuff much more than I do."

"You wish she was here with you?"

I make a face, like I'm not bothered either way, but my heart clenches to let me know it thinks I'm a big liar. Museums, art — that's much more Lara's type of thing than mine, and the reason the Louvre was first on the itinerary was because I was counting on her to guide me through it. I was counting on her to know what Mom and Dad connected with twenty-five years ago. Lara was supposed to tell me what they saw in this place. Without her, I'm feeling nothing, except a sadness and a sort of *shame* that I'm feeling nothing. This place meant something to Mom and Dad — it was special. But why?

Once the scrapbook is finished, I tell myself, *then it'll be different. And it will be good for Lara and Mom to have something, too. This way, we won't have to try so hard to hold on to our memories of ...*

I still can't finish that thought.

"Then perhaps we should see all the pieces as quickly as possible," Jean-Luc says, gesturing down the corridor, "and get out of here?"

He's got a focused look on his face, and his hands are fussing at the camera around his neck. As if, for all his talk of being "moved" by the art, he's remembered that he left his dorm with a project to finish, and even the Louvre is just a hindrance.

He walks hurriedly past me, and I shake my head.

All of a sudden, I'm slowing *him* down!

✳

Five minutes later, we're back at ground level, walking through the Greek Antiquities exhibit toward where the *Venus de Milo* is housed. To get there, we pass a great many sculptures of what I guess are Greek people, whose only interests seemed to be posing naked or fighting — which they also apparently liked to do naked. The ceilings of the Louvre are high and arched, and they seem to trap the constant murmuring, in many languages, throwing it around the room like a game of voice racquetball. I'm not annoyed by it, though — I kind of hope that all the noise will fill my head and drive back the thoughts that are fighting their way to the front of my mind. Thoughts about Dad. Questions about how happy he was here, the day he visited with Mom. The wondering, was he always that happy? Was he happy the day he … got into his car …? I screw my eyes shut and shake my head, as if I can throw these thoughts, these questions, right out of it. As I do this, I make eye contact with Jean-Luc, and I feel a stab of panic that he's going to ask me what's on my mind, and that when he does, I might actually *tell him*, which would be bad because I'm not sure I can do that without crying.

But he doesn't ask me what's on my mind, doesn't make a sympathetic face and ask if I'm okay. His deep brown eyes just regard me as we walk, as if he's waiting to see if I'm going to tell him why I suddenly, like, shivered. When I say nothing, he just looks away, and I feel oddly grateful not to have to explain myself.

"These hallways go on forever," I huff, as we weave in and out of clusters of people. Everyone takes up twice as much space as they might in the summer, due to all the winter coats. "Reminds me of those really old cartoons — you know, like, from the eighties and stuff, when characters would be chased down hallways, and you'd see the same things over and over again because the animators had only drawn one or two pieces of furniture."

Jean-Luc smiles. "It's how I imagine purgatory," he says. "A space that looks like it goes on forever but actually goes nowhere."

Wait a minute — is he saying that being with me is like being in purgatory?

We turn to walk under an arch, and the Lady Venus is instantly visible, standing with her side to us. Seeing her from this angle, so abruptly, makes it hard to feel any wonder at seeing her for the first time. There was no warning, no sign saying, "Be ready, because there's Great Art in five ... four ... three ..." It's just ... there! The tourists — not quite as many as at the *Mona Lisa* but still a good number — are gathered in front of or to either side of the broken statue.

Slowly, we move around to the front, accidentally photo-bombing at least six selfies. Once we're there, I look up at the statue, and the first thing I notice is not the severed arms or the exposed breasts or the strange posture — what I notice first is something that I'd never really registered all the times I'd looked at photographs of the *Venus de Milo*.

"She's got *abs*." I mumble this to Jean-Luc, and he gives me another look, as if to say: "Seriously?" I shrug and tell him: "I'm just saying. How'd all those Ancient Greeks and Romans get so fit? It's not like there were gyms in every village. I run twice a week, and my body fat has *never* been as low as what I'm seeing here. I mean, is it any wonder so many of them were — apparently — super cool with being painted or sculpted naked?" It's a stupid thought, from a person who maybe isn't taking the Louvre as seriously as she should be, but it feels like *just* the sort of discussion Mom and Dad would have had when they were here. Mom's so practical, she probably saw the *Venus de Milo* and felt sorry for whichever poor saps had to carry it from place to place.

She probably worried about them getting in trouble for dropping it and breaking her arms.

And what would Dad have said in response? He'd have reassured her, said, no way they'd have gotten in serious trouble, not once people got a look at the broken statue. With her arms, she's just a normal woman; without them, she's *unique*. Yeah, Dad probably said something like that, because Dad never wanted to think negatively about anything. Mom would have laughed, because she always laughed when Dad was so resolutely upbeat. Sometimes, she laughed because she loved his positivity; other times she laughed because she thought he was (the best kind of) silly.

But the point was, she laughed. They made each other laugh. Gave each other joy.

I steal a look at Jean-Luc, while he's gazing at Venus, see his very serious, thoughtful face, so serious and thoughtful I find it hard to imagine him ever laughing the way I remember Mom and Dad laughing. In fact, I think the only time I've seen him smile today was when he said being at the museum with me was like being in purgatory.

I turn back to Venus. Man, how could some sculptor — working more than two thousand years ago — carve a totally lifelike human being out of marble when, in the twenty-first century, I sometimes need two tries to get my eyeliner on right?

*

After I've swung by a bust of a satyr with a really creepy smile (Mom and Dad always did seem to find the weirdest things funny), I have gotten every photo I came here to get. I am officially ready to move on to the next stop on the tour — Shakespeare and Company. And, of course, Jean-Luc has wandered off again. Seriously, it's like having an overgrown, very serious toddler — okay, he might have an enjoyable accent, but he's not exactly the best person to have around you when you're trying to keep to a schedule. Although, I do kind of like the fact that he doesn't talk down to me about stuff — even when I'm asking him, for the eighth time, "Is that baby supposed to be Jesus? Are those guys the musketeers?" Besides, if he wasn't here, I'd just be a girl walking around by herself, sometimes looking a little confused, other times crying. It's not what it would have been like had Mom or Lara been with me, but I am kind of glad Jean-Luc decided to tag along this morning.

I turn a one-eighty and find him creeping up on an elderly couple sitting on a bench, holding hands. I sidle up to him and hiss: "What are you *doing?*"

He startles. Doesn't say *"mon dieu!"* or *"sacré bleu!,"* like I'm expecting him to. But he does give me a look as if to say, "Please don't do that again." He turns away as he checks the camera's little preview screen on the back, nods to himself, then looks at me. "You get your last photo?" he asks.

I tell him I have, figuring he's not going to tell me what he was doing …

He just nods again. "Then we can go."

I have to jog to catch up to him. I say thanks for the tour, just to have something to say. When I see him fiddling with his camera again, I feel a flash of guilt at how I'm maybe getting in his way.

He does have a project to finish, after all. "I can take it from here, though, if you need to finish up your work." *But I hope you don't,* I add silently. *I hope you stay.*

"I am happy to keep walking," he says. It's hard to tell if he's being sarcastic. Maybe he is. Or maybe he is just being blunt. He could also be making a more general point about life itself.

Then he goes on. "Just as long as we don't walk too fast, okay?"

I bite back my response that walking fast is kind of essential when you're trying to cross off stops on a tour. Although, I doubt Mom and Dad were running around when they were here. They would've just been excited to be in Paris, with the person they loved, not some moody French dude who may or may not like them all that much.

I might be walking in Mom and Dad's literal footsteps, but I am *not* going to be able to have their experience. I have a brief flash of despair — literally the one thing the Romance Tour *won't* be is romantic, so can I really hope to truly understand what this city meant to my parents? Should I have abandoned this whole little mission as soon as Lara told me she was double-booked and had to go to Madrid with Henri?

No. Because, Mom will love the scrapbook I make for her, once it's finished, and I'm determined to leave here having figured out a thing or two about what love really is.

Once we're back outside, I turn up my collar to guard as much of my face as possible from the winter chill.

"So," he says, "to the Left Bank? Shakespeare and Company?"

It's not my mouth that replies, but my stomach. It suddenly gives a loud rumble that seems to go on forever.

Jean-Luc raises his eyebrows. They're kind of perfectly shaped. I wonder if this is European genetics or if he has them done professionally. It would be kind of weird if he got them done professionally, right? Or maybe that's just the "unenlightened American" in me talking. "Perhaps, instead, somewhere for breakfast?"

I feel blood creeping up into my cheeks. "Oh, it's cool, I can just scarf a candy bar or something while we walk over the bridge."

He makes a face at me like he's not impressed. It's not the first time I've seen this expression in the less than two hours I've known him. "If you are to have fuel for the rest of the day, you need *real* food. Not your processed junk. I'll take you to a café."

"But I don't have time —"

"I do not think your parents starved themselves twenty-five years ago. If you pass out from hunger, you'll miss everything else on your list. You must eat. Come, follow me."

Which I do, grudgingly grateful that he's leading me back across Pont du Carrousel. We'll at least be on the Left Bank, so we won't be getting *farther* away from Shakespeare and Company, and my rumbling belly is quite happy about this unscheduled detour.

~ CHAPTER FOUR ~
JEAN-LUC

12H05

I'm glad I got to spend an hour in the Louvre, even though it was strangely lacking in inspiration for me. Too many of my shots were invaded by tourists taking selfies with their backs to the art — because, obviously, it is more important to record "I was here" than to connect with the artists' works. But perhaps most disappointing is the last photograph I got, of the old couple on the bench. When I took it, I thought I had perfectly captured their detachment from the museum around them, their frailty within the healthy, thriving culture — a culture which is time-less in a way that people are not — but now that I'm looking at it, I'm just bothered by how out of focus the museum is and how clear *they* are. It's basically just a photo of an elderly couple who could be holding hands in *any* room in *any* city in the world. That was not the point. My theme is supposed to be "Stories from Paris" — not "Stories of People Dying Slowly *in* Paris."

I look up from the camera to Serena on the other side of the table in the café. From the way her eyebrows are raised, I gather she must have asked me something.

"I am sorry," I say, putting the camera down. "I was distracted. What was the question?"

"How long have you lived in Paris? Your whole life?"

I shake my head. "Fourteen years. Before that, we lived with my father in New Jersey."

"Oh, really? What exit?"

I don't understand the question. I tell her this.

"You know, the New Jersey Turnpike," she says. "That never-ending toll road from Hell. It's in the opening credits of *The Sopranos*? Almost everyone in the state lives close to the Turnpike."

"I do not remember it," I say.

She seems shocked. "Seriously? What kind of Jersey Boy are you?"

"I suppose the exiled kind."

Serena laughs as a waitress comes over and takes our order, in English — probably because she heard us speaking it just now. Serena asks for a chocolate crêpe and an espresso. That sounds good, so I ask for the same.

When the waitress walks away, Serena turns back to me. "So I guess you grew up speaking English?"

I nod. "Until we came here, obviously. I have been bilingual pretty much since birth."

"I'm kind of jealous. I suck at learning new languages. How much do you remember about living in America?"

I shrug. "I have *some* memories, but they're … muddled. The type of memories that could be real or could just be memories of things that other people have told me. But, to be honest, I try not to remember America all that much." She makes an offended face — it might be sarcasm, but I don't know her well enough to take the chance, so I jump in to clarify: "Because of my father, not the country. He was … not nice to my mama. I think he didn't really want children — back then — and so was kind of always in a bad mood, you know? I remember my mother being sad, all the time."

"He sounds kind of selfish," she says.

"Yeah, that's it exactly," I tell her, nodding. "He's selfish."

She's narrowing her eyes at me, her lips curling in a slow smile. "What is it?" I ask.

"No, nothing," she says, "just … there're times when I can really hear an American accent trying to fight its way out of you."

She's smiling, like she thinks this is kind of cool — something that we have in common. I try not to let my annoyance show — even Mama occasionally likes to say that when we moved to Paris, we left behind everything but my accent. Since meeting Lara at the beginning of this semester, nasal vowels have started to escape my lips more than I like.

But I am *not* American. The only American in my life left long ago.

Serena's peering at me. "You don't talk much, huh?" she says.

Hmm. How long have I been silent? "That depends on who you're comparing me to," I say.

Her brow furrows, and I realize — too late — she thinks I am being unkind to her. Just then, the waitress comes back with our order, and when the clinking of plates and confusion of putting everything in its place is over, I feel awkward bringing up my silence again. When the waitress moves on, Serena picks up her espresso and turns to her side, facing the café as if she's ending our interaction altogether.

"Excuse me for trying to make conversation," she mumbles in between blowing on her coffee.

I could clarify that that isn't what I meant, but something about what she just said irritates me. "*Making conversation* is what I tried to do when we were by the pyramid, but you wanted to get into the Louvre. Now, because I do not want to discuss weather, I am bad guy?" I may or may not be deliberately breaking my own English.

"I didn't say anything about the weath —"

"Just because I do not talk so much, this does not mean I am not here. I think Americans must be, oh, what is the word" — I know what the word is, I don't know why I'm pretending I don't — "allergic to silence. You are scared of it. My father, when he calls me, he talks only about the weather, the price of airfare, what he should send me for Christmas. And he is spending money to do this, when he could be asking about ..."

Despite the anger I'm feeling, I still can't bring myself to finish *that* sentence. I look at the walls, at a framed photograph of a motionless, tranquil Seine River. I stare at it, as if I might be able to absorb some of its calm. I see the way Serena's peering at me, as if she's asking me, what is my problem?

I *am* being unkind to Serena, allowing a normal conversation to become "spirited" far too easily. Maybe this is a reflex, after

Martine and all the impassioned arguments that were so frequent they became normal. Thinking of her seems to add weight to the cell phone in my jacket pocket. I expect I'll see at least one missed call when I next check it.

Serena is still staring at me through the faint, spiraling curls of steam rising off her espresso. I get an urge to take her picture, but even I am not so dense about women that I cannot see this would be a bad idea. She makes a *tut* sound, looks down at the coffee. The silence is like an invisible hand on the back of my head, pushing it down. I do the only thing I know to do in awkward silences — I pick up my camera. I flick through the photos that I have taken so far today and try not to shake my head. It's hard not to. There's plenty of people in my photos, but maybe not enough of the city to make Monsieur Deschamps happy. And, looking at them, I don't really know what their "stories" are.

I stop on a picture of Serena. She's staring at a painting, and her eyes are bright and alive with ... something.

I turn the camera to show her. "Do you know what you were thinking here?"

She is wiping her hands on a napkin after finishing her crêpe. She stares at the photo on the preview screen for a couple of seconds. From the way her eyes flicker, judder back and forth, I know that she's trying to locate the memory. "I didn't notice you taking this."

"I am sorry."

"No, it's okay," she says, never taking her eyes off the photo. "This was when I was looking at this painting, it was ... Yeah, it was David holding Goliath's severed head. Kind of gross, but it was one of the pieces in the Louvre that I actually *got*. I knew it would be something my dad would have liked. He loved stories like that — you know, combat and stuff? Heroism, underdogs … When I was little, he never read me girlish books about fairies or angels. He'd tell me stories about heroes and warriors — David and Goliath, Daniel in the Lions' Den. This painting reminded me of him, of how it felt to be close to him. It was … a nice feeling."

She stares into the distance for a second. Then she closes her eyes and shakes her head, as if resetting herself — not wanting to cry. She gestures at the camera, as if to ask if she can look through the pictures. I sit back in my chair. "Of course."

The tension between us is draining away, and I am relieved. "I like some of these," she says. "How long have you been interested in photography?"

This is actually not easy to answer, because — strangely — I do not get asked this question often. "Definitely since I was a child," I tell her. "Mama says that I once told her I never wanted to forget anything for the rest of my life, and so I figured the only way to do that would be to take photographs of everything."

"And you haven't stopped since?"

"I guess not. Although, I do not take photos of *everything* anymore." I feel a flush creep into my cheeks. I'm a little embarrassed by what I'm about to say, because I know it sounds kind of sappy. "I like to know that the memories are there for me. If I want to relive something, I can sort of do it, you know?"

I see her staring at me and know she has a follow-up question. But I don't think my cheeks can flush any more without exploding, so instead I say, "So, Lara said you're at Columbia, right? Have you chosen your major yet?"

She drains her coffee. Shrugs at me. "Physics ... or Math. I'm still making up my mind."

"That is your passion?" My face must show my surprise, because she rolls her eyes at me.

"Yes. People can get excited by things that *aren't* artistic, you know?"

"I do, I do. Sorry, I did not mean to be insulting. What is it that you like about those subjects?"

"I like that, ultimately, your goal is to find an answer to a problem. And when you find it, the answer is the answer — it's indisputable. Physics and Math aren't messy. Well, Physics can be, but you know what I mean, right?"

I kind of don't, but her eyes have a light in them now. I want her to keep talking, but she has turned her attention back to my camera.

"Are these all photos you've taken today?" she asks. I nod. "You've taken a *lot* — you like to leave your homework to the last minute, huh?"

I quickly take another bite of my crêpe, so that I couldn't answer even if I wanted to. I can do nothing about the memory that marches through my mind, though. The memory of looking at exactly forty-four photos and realizing just how mediocre they are.

As I finish my crêpe, Serena's eyes flash, showing interest, and I know instantly what she's looking at ... Before she has turned the camera around so I can see the preview screen, the blood is racing up into my cheeks, my shoulders hunching up by my ears, my eyes going back to that photo of the Seine on the wall. I feel like I could jump into it.

"Who is *she*?"

The photo is maybe a month old. Martine is reclining on the same chaise longue where Serena was sitting this morning. A shaft of light stabs through the dorm room window, turning her flame-colored curls into more of a blood-red, matching the tattoo she'd gotten the day before — a raven, suspended in flight, on the underside of her forearm.

I reach for the camera, but Serena leans back, holding it high and away from me. "Careful with that, please," I tell her. "It is very expensive."

"Is this your girlfriend?" she asks.

"She was."

"What happened?"

"She became my ex-girlfriend."

At first, I worry that my answer might make her angry again, but she just grins at me and goes back to flicking. "Okay, guess you don't want to talk about it."

She's right. I do *not* want to talk about Martine.

"Oh, now, this one I like!" She's turning the photo around so I can see it — the elderly couple, holding hands. I lean on the table to join her in looking.

"Really? You like that one?"

She makes a face at me, as if to ask if I'm being serious. "Yeah, it's great. The way the Louvre is out of focus, like their love for each other makes a famous museum seem irrelevant." She says this like she thinks that's what I was *trying* to capture. I'm about to correct her and tell her all the ways in which the photo is failing the assignment Monsieur Deschamps has given me, when ...

I see it. I see them. The way they hold hands lightly, secure in themselves, neither one fearing the other will suddenly leave, run away. My own hands instinctively flex, remembering how Martine would hold on to my hand so tightly my fingers would tingle with pins and needles for a long time after she let go. Serena has a point — I may not have intended to capture the moment, but I would be a fool to ignore it.

"You have a good eye," Serena tells me. I have to clench the muscles in my jaw to keep from smiling too broadly.

"So do you, to see so much meaning," I tell her, trying not to sound surprised that there is more substance to her than I expected. I should not be so quick to judge people, simply because they're from America! And if Serena can find this much meaning in my work, then ... "Maybe you'd like to come with me to my favorite art gallery. The street photography — it is *magnifique*. And it is currently running an exhibition of work by Noémie Dugarry. You may not have heard of her, but she is amazing."

Serena looks at her watch, realizes she's not wearing one, then reaches into her jacket for her cell phone. I see a folded piece of paper, which I know is a copy of her itinerary. I feel a twinge of disappointment. I barely know this American girl, and a good portion of our interaction has been strained — yet, I want her to be as excited by the exhibit as I am.

"Trust me." I'm actually leaning across the table while talking. "Her work will show you why so many people love this city.

And" — I gesture at the camera she was so keen to look through just now — "you clearly have an appreciation for photography. I really think you'll like it."

She looks at her phone, then at the piece of paper. Then she gives me a wary smile. "If you promise we can go straight to Shakespeare and Company afterward — remember, there's something I need to get — then sure. Why not?"

✱

13H10

Unlike the Louvre, there are *no* tourists in the Maison de la Photographie on rue des Saint-Pères. In fact, the only other person here is the owner, behind the counter — a man in a tatty tweed jacket that looks like it has never been washed. (Smells like it, too.)

The place is so deserted, the running commentary I am giving Serena on the Dugarry display sounds as though it's coming through speakers. My voice rebounds off the walls and, ordinarily, I'd cringe at the volume. But I can't help talking about how much I like her work, how much she inspired me when I first started thinking that photography was what I wanted to do. "Look at this," I say, pointing to a photo of a tired-looking mother watching her toddler chasing a runaway tennis ball in a playground. The mother's out of focus, the youngster's in sharp focus and the yellow tennis ball is the only flash of color in the black-and-white image (as if the parent is watching her own childhood run away, while her present becomes drab, colorless). "This is just a park in some random part of Paris, and yet — to me — this is a shot that could *only* be taken here. It is the people who make a city ... does that make sense?" She nods, and her eyes light with amusement at how passionately I am speaking. I feel the need to deflect. "You know, it probably wasn't a good idea for me to come here. Duggary's work is so far ahead of mine, simple and beautiful in its composition that it makes me a little bit angry. No matter how hard I try, I can't quite capture the truth the way that she does."

"Maybe it's Paris," Serena says. "Maybe you're too close to it to really *see* its truth? Sometimes, when something is right there in front of you, you end up seeing through it, you know what I mean? Like, how I totally noticed what was going on in that photo of the old couple before you did."

I snort, look at the ground. It seems she saw through *me* and knew instantly that all the stuff going on in that photograph was *not* my intention.

"You might be right," I concede. "Even a great city like this, you can take it for granted if it's around you every day. You forget to see it. It is amazing, *non*?" I wonder if, subconsciously, I am thinking about Martine here — how my heart suddenly seemed to just ... *forget* how passionate we were for each other.

"I revise my earlier comment," she says. "You *do* talk. Must be your American half, huh?"

I smile through my annoyance because I'm not all that annoyed. "If we're talking about photography, art, you will start wanting me to shut up. I have a lot to say. I just wish that I could produce the kind of work that people want to talk about."

She points at the camera around my neck — it's starting to feel a little bit heavy to me now. "Hey, it might have been an accident, but still — there was heart in that shot of the old couple. It's not like you *can't* do it."

"Fantastic," I mumble, looking back to the exhibit. "Now I must hope for more accidents."

There is a sudden flare of light that almost gives *me* a heart attack, a red-green glare like graffiti on my vision.

"No photos!" the owner calls out, in French. Serena lets the hand holding her phone drop to her side, raising her other hand in what I think is supposed to be an apology — but her expression is not sorry at all.

"Thank you for bringing me here," she tells me. "The photos are great. I see why you like this place so much. But do you mind if we get going? I need to reconfigure my itinerary for the rest of the day."

She's looking at me with an energy that makes me vow to intervene if she tries to order any more espressos.

I lead her out of the gallery and back onto the street. The icy December wind is blade-sharp, and we both pull our coats tighter around ourselves. On the street, a taxi begins to slow down, mistaking us for fares. It speeds up and drives on by when my hands go into my pockets. On its side is an ad for a supermarket chain, with what looks like three generations of relatives around a dining table — the point apparently being that dinnertime is *extra* important for families in late December.

Maybe it is. But I know for a fact that, while there *will* be three generations of family sitting around our Christmas table this year, the scene will not be quite so happy.

Serena is staring at me — well, she's staring at the picture of me that she has on her phone. She turns the screen around so I can see it. "I know I'm not a real photographer," she says, "but I think this is pretty nice. I'd gotten so used to seeing you look serious and scowly that, when a real smile broke through and stayed there, I just … had an urge to capture it."

I look at the photo. There's me, almost in profile, staring at Noémie Dugarry's work but not seeing it, the corner of my mouth just starting to rise, because at that second I was imagining sneaking up on people and taking their pictures.

I find myself agreeing with her — it is a good photo. And it makes me wonder … how long has it been since I've smiled like that?

~ CHAPTER FIVE ~

SERENA

1:46 P.M.

As I lock my phone to put it back in my coat pocket, I see that it's now 1:46 p.m.! And the only thing I've crossed off my itinerary is the Louvre. I'm almost regretting *eating*, even though that crêpe was the best thing I've eaten in, I don't know, maybe forever.

I should have broken away from Jean-Luc when we left the Louvre, but he looked so keen to show me *his* gallery, so certain that I'd have a *reaction* to the photos there, that I didn't have the heart to tell him no. And I did like the photos that were on display — I will admit that — this Noémie Dugarry lady *is* some kind of genius. But now, the only way I will catch up with my itinerary is if I somehow get my hands on a time machine.

"Hey, can you tell me which Metro station I need to get to Shakespeare and Company?" I ask him.

"It is not far," he says, gesturing that I should follow him down the street. "You don't need the Metro."

He has his back to me, so he doesn't notice that I throw up my hands. "It'll be faster to take the Metro, though, right?"

"The tunnels do not have the *Seine*." I don't know if it's his accent that makes him sound like he's constantly disapproving or if he finds my wanting a convenient, fast method of travel offensive.

"I am certain," he goes on, "that your parents took a walk along the river."

I catch up to my "guide," grateful for my sneakers, even though I've caught him giving them a snooty look on more than one occasion since we left his dorm. But I don't care, because I've done a lot of walking already today, and my feet aren't telling me to quit it. Comfort over fashion — always. "Oh, they did more than that. They took a tour boat — my dad told me. It's just that I have a very specific list of places that I need to see and get pictures of, and I'm losing time."

He grins at me, turning and walking away — I hope in the direction of the bookstore! "Just for you, we walk fast!"

✳

Jean-Luc is gesturing as we walk along the broad stone walkway on the banks of the Seine. I know from my guidebooks that it's called Quai Saint-Michel. Notre-Dame Cathedral looms on the other side of the river, very grand and very gothic. Even ghostly, because it's shrouded in the fog. "You must be happy you get to see this?"

It's hard to tell if he's asking me a question or *instructing* me on how to feel. I mean, the cathedral does look great and all — and I have no idea how people pulled off building something like that nearly a thousand years ago — but it's hard for me to appreciate its architecture when all I can think about is: Will I ever get to Shakespeare and Company?

Aaaand now Jean-Luc has stopped, falling back to take a photo of … something. I think it's one of the cars crawling along the street — traffic in this part of Paris is almost as bad as Midtown Manhattan. He's even *crouching,* and a hot flush of embarrassment swells in my face (the feeling so sharp I almost wince). It's as if *I'm* the local and he's the tourist, discovering the city for the first time.

"Hey!" I call out, digging through my brain for the words for "my friend." I think it's — "*Mon frère!* What is the French word for 'itinerary'?"

He's laughing now — and I don't know why, but when he does, it makes me want to go over to him and kick him with my orange sneakers, right into the river he was so keen to walk along.

"What's so funny?"

He straightens up and walks over to me, still cracking up. "I did not know I had an American sister."

I will my face not to catch fire. The blush is equal parts embarrassment — of course "*frère*" is French for "brother"! — and fury, because, damn it, I hate being *behind schedule!*

I shove my hands into my pockets, so that my anger doesn't get the better of me. It's been so long since I really and truly yelled at someone, I'm not entirely sure what I'd do. Wave my arms? Pull at my hair? I just don't know …

I don't know what to do with these feelings.

What's worse, the corner of my itinerary — which lost all meaning an hour ago — cuts at my bare fingers. I left my gloves in my suitcase, like an idiot. Everything's going wrong! "Not that I'm trying to rush you or get in your way, but I'd like to keep moving — I have the bookstore, then Montmartre, the Arc de Triomphe, and the Champs-Élysées —"

He just looks at me. "This is too much for one day, *non*? Even with those terrible shoes, your feet will blister. And, believe me, you will regret this trip if you do not get to really *see* Paris."

I don't know if I'm just too tired to argue with him, or if he's talked about *seeing Paris* so much today that he's finally gotten through to me, but I'm starting to think he might have a point. When we were in the Louvre, I *was* starting to feel a little frustrated moving from one piece of art to the next so quickly. It's all well and good ticking off sights on a piece of paper, but that's not the same as *really experiencing* them, is it? Mom and Dad had a whole honeymoon here, and maybe that's why it meant so much to them — they would have had time to wander, they would have stopped, sat and talked. They would have held hands as they let this most romantic of cities become a part of them, of their connection. They didn't come back from Paris with just a bunch of photos. They came back with memories that, years later, they still talked about — remembering how they felt, what they said to each other.

What will I talk about when I'm older? How will I describe *my* time in Paris to people? I'll be able to say where I was and what I did, and I'll have the photographs to prove it — prove that I was here — but what will I say to anyone who asks me, how was Paris?

What if my only answer to that question is to hand them my phone and say, "Take a look"?

I don't want *that*. I want to go home and feel like Paris is a special place to *me*, too. And Jean-Luc is right, it is people who make a city. It would be nice to experience a strange city *with* someone, even if that someone's a stranger.

"You're right," I tell him, taking out my pen — which feels more like an ax that I'm about to take to my itinerary. "I'll just pick, like, the top five or so and make sure I hit them. Five spots should give me enough material for the scrapbook."

"Scrapbook?" he asks. He sounds like he wants to hear more about it, but I'm too busy putting lines through certain places, question marks beside others. I'm sure that, if I had asked her, Mom would have told me which sights were her favorites, but I never asked her. What if I'm crossing off something that Mom considers essential?

The only thing I will absolutely not cross off, though:

"The Eiffel Tower. Whatever else happens, I *have* to be at the Eiffel Tower for ten p.m. — what?"

Jean-Luc's got another one of his faces on — not snooty this time but definitely concerned about something. "You have a ticket, yes? I am not certain, but … I think tonight, there's a big firework and light show. For the winter season. Very expensive, very, uh …" He clicks his fingers, searching for the English.

I skip to the end. "They're sold out? Oh, don't worry about that. I have my ticket" — and my sister's and mom's — "which I booked ages ago." I don't tell him about how stressful it was, booking these tickets. The light show seemed to make the Eiffel Tower more popular than ever, and the website said that every day in December only had three or four tickets left. I'm sure it'll be great, and everything, but I'm not here for a light show! I tuck my itinerary under one arm, then use the other to rummage in my cross-body bag to prove it. I fumble around a little but feel only my guidebook and maps, the empty clear plastic folder that I kept my Louvre tickets in ... but not the one that has my tickets for the tower. I kneel down so I can dig deeper, but just because I can now see into my bag does not mean the tickets will suddenly be there.

Actually, they are gone.

A memory comes to me — turbulence early in the flight, right around the time we were flying over Newfoundland. The plane shaking like it was having a seizure, and my tote bag ... it was under my seat, and I noticed at the end of the flight that it was ... upside down? It was knocked over by the turbulence ... My tickets to the tower must have fallen out! Oh God, are they still on the plane? Can I head back to the airport and pick them up? No, that's crazy — my plane is probably heading back to New York by now. And it would have been cleaned right after we deboarded, which means that probably a member of the airline crew picked them up. Maybe they have them right now. Maybe they're thinking, "Why not? Free trip!" Could I head them off at the tower, explain the situation and ask for my tickets back?

You're being crazy, Serena. The tickets don't even have your name on them, so how are you going to prove they're yours?

My eyes sting with tears of fury. Of all the disasters I've suffered today, this is the absolute worst!

Jean-Luc has one hand at the back of his neck, like he's very uncomfortable watching me get emotional. "What's wrong?"

I look at him, shaking my head. "They're gone," I say, staggering to my feet. "The tickets. The tickets I've had for *months*."

Jean-Luc looks sincerely upset for me. "I am sorry this has happened."

I *had* to get to the Eiffel Tower. Dad really wanted to take a trip up to the top, but they never made it. It was the one thing he never got to show my mom, the one thing … My heart feels like it's trying to crawl up out of my mouth so it can go for a swim in the Seine. My belly churns like I might throw up, my fists clench, and I feel like I could quite happily stomp on my cross-body bag, reducing all the useless itineraries inside it to the trash that they are at this point. The great day I had planned for (what's left of) my family has been reduced to me, stranded in Paris, kind-of sort-of abandoned by said family and unable to do the *one thing* on my itinerary that I absolutely, positively did not want to miss.

I stagger over to a bench facing the Seine and put my face in my palms. *Why didn't I think to double-check my bag as I left the plane?*

I feel Jean-Luc take a seat next to me. His hand falls lightly on my shoulder.

"What is so important about the tower?" he asks me.

I part the heels of my hands so I can talk through the gap. "My parents never actually made it there. It was the one thing they really wanted to do on their honeymoon, and they missed it." I've never actually heard the story of why, but they did.

"But I thought you wanted to see only the places your parents saw on their trip?"

"I did … I do …" I wipe away the tears, sit back and sniffle. Out of the corner of my eye, I can see Jean-Luc staring at me. His hand is still on my shoulder. I stare out to the Seine — a tour boat passes by, cutting a wound in the surface of the water that disappears within seconds. I wish I could heal myself as quickly as the river does.

"I wanted to finish the trip *for* them," I tell him. "I know that it always bugged them a little that they came all the way to Paris for their honeymoon only to miss the Eiffel Tower of all things. My dad mentioned it once, that it was a big regret of his and that — one day — he wanted to make it up to my mom."

I steal a glance at him and brace myself to say the words I've not said in two years, because — of course — he's going to want to know why Dad can't just bring Mom here himself. But his deep brown eyes are warm, narrowed in what looks like understanding. It's the same look he had in the Louvre, as we walked to the *Venus*, and I realize that Lara must have mentioned something at some point since they met. I'm relieved I get to skip that part of the explanation.

"My parents' wedding anniversary is on New Year's Day," I tell him. "It would have been twenty-five years. I was going to give my mom a scrapbook, her daughters and her in some of those special places, all the photographs building to a shot of us at the Eiffel Tower. Like, through us, a part of Dad finally made it there, you know? I felt like I would be helping him keep his promise to Mom. Then Mom goes and gets called away on some conference in London — she's an economics professor, so that kind of thing happens a lot — and then Lara decides she'd rather go to Madrid, but still … I'm a part of my dad, and I could get up there for him and get a photo. I've never been so psyched to take a selfie in my life! And today is the one day I don't obsessively check …"

I let my words collapse into a growl — if I don't, I might start crying again — and look back to the river.

"Maybe I should just call all of this off. I mean, the tower was kind of the whole point, and if I can't get there —"

"What about tomorrow?" Jean-Luc's fingers relax, start to creep across my back, then return to their original position, like he thought about putting his arm around me and changed his mind. "*La tour* Eiffel is not going to disappear."

I shake my head. "I'd still need a ticket to get up there tomorrow, and I think it's pretty much totally sold out right through New Year's. Plus, I've got to get to Gare du Nord at one in the afternoon to catch a Eurostar to London that leaves at two. I'm going to be meeting my mom there. Jeez, what a disaster …"

When I look at him again, I'm almost startled — he hasn't moved at all. His eyes are staring straight into mine. He looks both curious and like he's pitying me. I feel a sudden prickle of self-consciousness — explaining the reasons for my trip in all this detail makes me realize that the trip is actually a little …

"Morbid. That's what you're thinking, right?" I ask. "What kind of eighteen-year-old comes to Paris to recreate her *parents' honeymoon*?"

The kind who is out of ideas about how to get over losing her dad and willing to fly 3,624 miles to see if a special city might do the trick.

"I do not think this." He lifts his hand off my shoulder, looks to the ground. Pondering something. "It is good to remember."

"Hah!" The sound I make is completely without humor. "Given how big a disaster this trip has been so far, I'm kind of hoping I get a concussion that wipes the last five hours from my brain." I turn away from him, stare at the Seine and shake my head — at what, I don't really know. Paris? Myself?

Click-click.

I whip my head to the right, staring straight into the lens of the camera that he is lowering.

"*Pardon*," he says, at least having the decency to blush a little. "Just so beautiful ... I mean, the *moment* was beautiful. The city behind you, the sadness on your face — not that I am happy you're sad, but ... err ..."

His face has gone from pink to tomato-red. I am about to put him out of his misery, but he turns the camera to me so I can see the preview screen. There I am in the foreground, staring out to the river and the city. The cathedral is in soft focus, as if it's trying not to disturb my quiet, contemplative, personal moment, hanging back out of respect for my sadness.

"Feels pretty appropriate," I tell him. "My body is in one of the world's greatest cities, but my mind is elsewhere."

He lets his camera hang on his chest again, smiling at me as his complexion returns to normal. "Then we should walk."

We get off the bench and I go pick up my bag. I look around, about to ask him which of the remaining items on my itinerary is near here, when I catch a glimpse of something a little way along the sidewalk. Stalls, overlooking the river. They are covered in

Christmas decorations that look older than the two of us.

"What's this?" I ask him. "Some kind of street market?"

"Kind of," he says. "The vendors are here every day, for the tourists. You are hungry again? Looking for food?"

"No," I lie. As fabulous as that crêpe was, it's hardly going to keep me going when my belly is trying to figure out why it's craving breakfast at lunchtime. "Just … I'm wondering if they sell scarves. One of my dad's most favorite photos of my mom is of her by a Parisian market stall, modeling the scarf he bought her. She still wears it, twenty-five years later." I'm walking toward the market now, Jean-Luc just behind me.

I pass a few vendors selling model Eiffel Towers, a few more with long tables of secondhand paperbacks. Here and there, artists sit huddled in thick winter coats, waiting for tourists to come and ask them to sketch their portraits. I stop by a stall that sells scarves and hats and gloves. I can tell Jean-Luc isn't impressed. His hands are in his pockets, because, apparently, there are no pictures worth taking here. I'm about to suggest we just turn around and leave, but then I see the next stall has a row of Eiffel Tower scarves — the tower a harsh black silhouette against a setting sun, with a kissing couple beneath the arch. It's *so* tacky, and it's the kind of thing that I know that my sister will laugh about for *days*.

"I'm gonna go buy it," I tell Jean-Luc. I think I hear him sigh as I walk over, but I'm too tickled by the tacky scarf and imagining how stubborn Lara will be about wearing it next semester, even in one of the fashion capitals of the world. One of the (many) things I love about my big sister: she likes to look good, but she also doesn't mind looking a little silly.

When I take down one of the scarves, I turn it over to look for a price tag. I don't see one, so I spin around to ask Jean-Luc for help, but he's not there. I turn a full circle, stepping away from the stall, when I'm assailed by a storm of French that actually makes me take a step back. The lady manning the stall points from the scarf, to me, to herself, her hippy-ish bracelets jangling like the rattling chains of a prison guard. That's probably my imagination — and the jet lag — but I know enough to know she thinks I'm trying to steal the scarf.

"No, no. I mean — *non, non.*" I think my attempt at a French accent lands me somewhere in Spain. And I don't even have Jean-Luc to translate because he isn't anywhere to be seen. Whatever photo he's gone to get had better be something prizewinning.

I turn back when I feel the scarf almost snatched from my hands. I really don't want to have a tug-of-war over it, and Seller Lady's voice is probably disrupting the service over at Notre Dame, but, for some reason, I'm not letting go of the scarf.

"I actually wanted to *buy* this from you!" I yelp, just as some French guy appears by my side. Out of the corner of my eye, I see him making a placating gesture with his hands, as he says something to the seller. I hear the word "*Américaine*" and gather he's putting the blame on my nationality.

I decide to be offended *after* I'm out of this situation.

Except this guy seems somehow … familiar. I break eye contact with the seller lady and look to see who has come to rescue me. I actually gasp when I take in the tall guy in a tan peacoat with faintly fashionable horn-rimmed glasses.

"*Ethan?*" For a split second, it feels so surreal to see someone I know here in Paris, I wonder if I'm asleep, dreaming this awkward encounter. Then I remember that I *did* know Ethan was coming here, because he told me all about it, in great detail. Apparently, if you book a three-day city break *just before* Christmas, you save, on average, forty-two percent on airfare. That's the kind of thing Ethan just knows.

He'd gone on to say he wondered, as someone who considers himself too rational to believe in coincidences, did it mean anything that we were both going to be in Paris at the same time?

This conversation happened right before what my dormmate, Charlotte, came to call the *kisstastrophe*.

"Hi, Serena." He still has his perfectly manicured hands raised in an *It's okay* gesture for the seller's benefit. His pale blond hair is only a shade or two darker — if that — than his perfect teeth, which he flashes in a smile at the woman. He says something in French — *he speaks French?* — and she relaxes her grip on the scarf.

Then he turns back to me. "I told her you want to buy it."

"I'm having second thoughts now," I grumble.

The seller says something else in French — it must be something outrageous, because not only does Ethan roll his eyes at her, he also throws up his hands …

… and says "Pffft!," which I'm pretty sure is French for "You gotta be kidding me, lady!"

"What?" I ask him. "What did she say?"

He actually places one hand on his belly, like he's about to erupt from laughter. He's a pre-law student back home, so I'm not surprised he can hold his own in an argument — but I don't think there's this much pantomime during class at Columbia. "She wants thirty euros." Ethan puts his free hand on my shoulder while he continues his haggling. I know the stakes are — probably — only about twenty bucks, give or take, but in French, it feels *so* much more consequential. Finally, he turns back to me, not taking his hand off my shoulder. "She's willing to take ten. I still think that's way too much, but you look like you really want this scarf?"

I nod, dig into my bag for money and hand it over. The seller takes it with a snort, then turns her back on me as if I was never here.

"Thanks," I say, as Ethan follows me a few steps away. Instinctively, I look around for Jean-Luc. I'm wondering why he didn't come running over when he saw me *wrestling for a scarf* — but Ethan moves to stand in front of me.

"Don't mention it," he says. "Any excuse to put my mediocre French to work."

"You sounded like a local to me."

He grins sheepishly. "Well, I've studied it since freshman year of high school," he said. "I thought it might help me with the ladies. 'Language of love' and all that."

I laugh politely. *Language of love. Right.* How could I forget?

He's smiling at me now, no longer sheepish. In fact, he seems to be beaming at getting me out of that silly jam with the vendor, all over a tacky scarf.

And I start to feel bad that all I can really think about right now is the *kisstastrophe.*

*

The last time I saw Ethan was on the final day of classes. I'd gone along to a Christmas party on campus, which was being hosted by some sophomore girl whose name I didn't know and never found out. I only went because my dormmate, Charlotte, bugged me to go, and I quickly regretted it, because, as soon as we were there, I realized why Charlotte had been so insistent. Ethan was at the party, and Charlotte thought he and I were a good match.

"You should give him a chance," she told me, after I'd made it clear I did *not* appreciate the scheming. "It's not like you're making your decision based on actual evidence, is it?"

She had a point — and, just like her, I could see how super-organized, never-misses-a-class me and super-organized, gets-started-on-essays-in-week-one Ethan were a good match. (If it had been the two of us taking the Romance Tour, I'd have ticked off more than the Louvre by now, that's for damn sure!) But that was on paper.

"Shouldn't I feel something?" I mumbled to Charlotte as we fought our way into the kitchen for drinks. Two football players were arm-wrestling over the breakfast bar, and I was concerned, from how red their faces were, that one of them was going to have an aneurysm.

"Only after you've actually *gone on* a date," Charlotte told me. "Anything you feel before that is not to be trusted."

And then, pretty soon, Ethan was making a beeline for me in the kitchen, his tall body so slender he seemed to pass through the crush of people unnoticed. The way the lights bounced off his horn-rimmed glasses *could* have made him look a bit like a super-hero but actually made him look more like a mad scientist. Of course, Charlotte instantly ditched me to go find her boyfriend, Anthony. (I mean, I get why she did — Anthony's a pretty cool guy — but ditching is still ditching.)

Ethan came and stood in front of me, casting a shadow by standing beneath one of the ceiling lights. He was at least four inches taller than the next tallest person at the party. His shoulders were hunched up by his ears, as though they were trying to restrain his gangly arms. He hadn't even said a word, and he was already blushing. "Hey ..."

"Hey," I said back. I started to ask if he was having fun but chose not to risk him thinking I was being sarcastic. It was a party, and he was Ethan — I knew he was not having fun.

"Quite a semester, huh?" He gestured at the drink I was holding. "I think you've more than earned that drink."

"This is just Diet Coke," I told him. His face reddened again, like he was super-mad at himself for assuming anything. And I must have felt bad, because I suggested to him that we move out of the noisy kitchen, into the hallway outside the dorm room, so that we could hear each other talk. Even though I had no idea what we'd actually talk *about*.

Less than a minute later, we came up with something.

"I'm going to be in Paris, *too*," he said, launching into an explanation of all the money I could have saved if I had shopped around a little.

"I'm organized," I told him with a smirk, "but I'm not psychotic."

He did not laugh at all. In fact, he started to defend himself, as if he thought I was being serious. I wanted to tell him to calm down, but I figured that would just make it worse, so I talked over him. (Flirting, it seems, is not really my thing.)

"No, it's a family trip," I told him — because, at that time, it still *was*. "We're all going to kind of relive our parents' honeymoon, so Mom can, like, reminisce, and we can be there with her while she does."

"So you're just going to take your mom to see a bunch of sights that she's already seen?"

His question — and the disbelieving look on his face — was like a punch. A soft punch, sure, but who *wants* to be punched? And unlike the conversation we'd just been having, *this time* he wasn't aware that he'd said anything wrong. Because he didn't blush, didn't stutter — he just kept talking. And that was the one thing I did *not* want him to do at that point.

"Doesn't sound like much of a vacation, Serena. You'll be traveling all the way to Europe, just to come away with sad memories?"

The noise from the party seemed to get louder and louder, echoing in my brain. I was grateful for it suffocating whatever it was that he said next, but that question — why would I do it? — was already taking root in my mind. I had to tell myself, he didn't mean to upset me the way he had. Maybe he was asking a question that my other friends *wanted* to ask but didn't dare.

When I had tuned back in, Ethan was still talking: "… if you have any time left over?"

I figured he was saying we should meet up in Paris. "Probably won't have time," I said, trying to keep my voice even. "The itinerary is pretty strict."

He smiled, as if he liked the sound of that. "Well, you know, keep in touch. Be great if we could."

"Yeah, sure."

"And maybe" — there was something in the way his voice rose on the last syllable that signaled even to me, with my severe lack of experience at this sort of thing, that he was thinking about Making a Move — "next semester, we could, you know … hang out a bit more. I think that would make a lot of sense. From both our perspectives."

He was looking right at me then, right into my eyes — he couldn't have held my gaze any more firmly if he had put both his hands on my face. Even I knew he was going to *lean in* — and I was going to *lean away* as far as I could …

Which turned out to be only a few inches, because I happened to have my back against a wall. Which my head rebounded off, my cheekbone clipping his chin … It was a miracle he didn't lose any of his luminescent teeth.

Like Charlotte said the next day, when we were talking about everything that happened at the party … Total *kisstastrophe!*

"Oh, gosh, Ethan, I'm so sorry," I told him, as he ran his fingertips over his chin. He was waving away my apology, like it was no big deal, but I could tell from the way that he was looking straight at the floor that he was even more mortified than I was.

We exchanged apologies and wished each other well in Paris, saying that we guessed we'd just see each other next semester.

Then I watched him walk down the hallway, his shoulders slumped, hand still rubbing his chin.

It was only once he was outside that I realized that I was in pain. I rubbed my cheek, wincing and hoping I wasn't going to get some kind of "shiner," and then went back into the party to find something to add to my Diet Coke. I *had* earned it by now.

I found Charlotte in the kitchen. She was sitting on a countertop next to Anthony, showing him pictures of London on her cell phone — part of her mission to convince him to go home with her in the summer.

Charlotte hopped off the counter when she noticed I was back. She clasped both my hands excitedly. "How did it go?"

"I head-butted him in the face."

Charlotte rolled her eyes. "You could have just turned him down!"

I laughed ruefully. "You know what? I really don't think Ethan's right for me."

Charlotte stared at me for a second, then shrugged to signal: *I'm done trying to convince you that you're wrong.*

I changed the subject by asking Anthony and her about their summer plans, then zoned out as I wondered how a smart, practical, mature guy like Ethan could feel so wrong to a smart, practical, mature girl like me. I wondered, was it because he didn't get why I wanted to walk in my parents' footsteps this Christmas? His confusion — the look on his face that kind of asked, was I for real? — made me, briefly, question if the Romance Tour was kind of lame, kind of silly.

The fact that Ethan couldn't get that made me wonder, was there any poetry — romance — in Ethan's soul?

Because I want to have poetry and romance in mine. I just have to figure out where to find it.

*

That was the last I thought about Ethan until he suddenly appeared: this new, confident, cosmopolitan version of himself. Here in Paris, I'm looking at Ethan 2.0 and wondering if I was too hasty after the *kisstastrophe*. He's not fidgeting with his glasses when he talks to me. I always thought that was his thing.

"You seem weirded out that I'm here," he says.

I flap a hand dismissively. "Jet lag. Plus, it's been a crazy morning."

"Want to talk about it?"

"I really, really do not." We laugh. "So, how's your trip going?"

"It's been kind of awesome so far." He gestures with his eyes: Do I want to go over to the bench just off the last market stall? I shrug yes, and we both walk over and sit down, facing each other. I have a view of the Seine and Notre-Dame to my right and have to force myself not to keep looking for Jean-Luc. I can't decide if I'm worried that he ditched me or worried that he might think I ditched him — but if Ethan 2.0 is still a little sensitive, a little shy, I worry how he'll react if some cool, good-looking French guy suddenly shows up.

"I was so efficient with my route yesterday," Ethan says, "that I even got through half of what I had planned for today. That means, I have only five things to do to meet today's schedule — I can actually take my time," he says.

"Ugh, I'm so jealous. I've had a total failure of efficiency on my trip. Due to a series of disasters beyond my control, I've only seen one thing on my itinerary so far. Plus, the whole Big Finish to my trip went out the window when I found out that I left my Eiffel Tower tickets on the plane."

He makes a sympathetic face. "Oh, man, that must have sucked. I know how long that online queue was — it took me an hour and thirty-seven minutes to get my tickets."

I've grabbed his arm before I've had time to really think if it's a good idea. "You have tickets? To the Eiffel Tower? Tonight, you have tickets?"

He's leaning back, and I cringe. I'm so excited, I've actually gotten *Ethan* to recoil from me! "Um, yeah," he says, through a nervous chuckle. "When I was researching what I was going to do, I saw that the display was tonight, so ..."

"You said 'tickets' — plural, right?"

He's making a face, like he doesn't like where this is going. Of course he doesn't like it — why would he want the *kisstastrophe-girl* tagging along? "I'm so sorry, but ... I kind of told my buddy Jesse that he could have the other ticket. I've known him since boarding school, and he's letting me crash in his dorm while I'm here, so I thought I'd better offer it to him."

"Oh." I force myself not to lean back and turn away from him *too* quickly, *too* decisively. I'm a little bummed out, but I'm not an asshole. Even if Ethan did have a spare ticket, it's not like I'd have any real *claim* to it. "Well, that should be fun."

"Yeah, it should be real romantic."

"Oh ..." I say again. I didn't know Ethan was bi.

Then I see him smiling at me. Sarcasm! I didn't know Ethan did *sarcasm.*

His face gets serious. "Listen, I know you, uh, got this whole ...

family thing going on, but if that itinerary of yours really is flexible, maybe we could meet up for coffee before you go to London. I expect to be free between six thirty and eight tonight."

I'm kind of impressed he doesn't even need to consult his schedule. Just as I'm reaching into my bag to find mine — trying not to laugh too bitterly at the fact that I'm even still consulting it — he's handing me a piece of paper.

"My cell works here," he says. "Here's my number, just in case you ... lost it."

I hope my face doesn't show that I did seriously consider deleting it after the *kisstastrophe*.

"In case there's any problems with cell coverage," he says, "I've put Jesse's number on there, too."

I accept the offer. "You think of everything," I say. I mean it as a compliment.

He smiles back at me. A few weeks ago, that pale complexion would have turned rose red, but now he's in Paris, traveling alone, bunking with friends, seeing the sights and haggling in French.

Was I wrong about the lack of poetry?

Ethan stands up and says that he really ought to get going, because he needs to be at the Musée d'Orsay in — he checks his watch — twenty-seven minutes. "Can't wait to see an *actual* Van Gogh!"

"Okay." I stand up, too, putting the paper with the phone numbers into my cross-body bag. "It was good to see you."

"It was good to see you, too." And now his left hand is lightly on my upper right arm, just the fingertips for a second, before he takes a firmer grip. His eyes are on mine, and I wonder if we have another *kisstastrophe* coming.

But it's just one of those European kisses — right cheek, then left. I guess Ethan's subscribing to the when-in-Rome philosophy. Except, you know, in Paris.

And then Ethan — or some confident, assured Europhile wearing his face — is gone, weaving his way through the street market toward the river.

"You found a friend."

Jean-Luc is suddenly beside me — standing very still, as if he's been there awhile. He's watching Ethan go, and because Jean-Luc's in profile, I can't tell if he's curious or upset. He may have a right to be, as I kind of ditched him just now. No, what am I saying? *He* just wandered off, while I was getting yelled at by some street vendor.

"Don't sneak up on me like that," I snap. "I don't want to get spooked and hit you over the head, or something. Think of the medical bills."

"In France, we have universal healthcare. I'd be well looked after." He turns his face to me now, and there's a gleam in his brown eyes. "Unlike in America."

"Just don't startle me like that, please. And I didn't 'find' a friend — that's actually someone I know from school back home."

Jean-Luc points to the bench where Ethan and I had been sitting. "Do not forget the scarf he bought you."

"He didn't buy it for me," I say, leaning down to scoop it up. I wrap it around my neck. "But he did make sure I had to pay only ten euros, when the lady wanted thirty."

Jean-Luc chuckles as he turns to walk away from the market. "Good for him," he says. "But it is not worth more than five."

~ CHAPTER SIX ~

JEAN-LUC

14H23

Once we're walking away from the stalls, I start to feel a bit bad about how I just treated Serena. As much as I'm trying to show her the real Paris, this is *her* trip, and I maybe shouldn't be getting in the way. But something happened when I turned back from taking a photo of a couple walking a dog that was almost as big as the two of them. I called out to Serena, to show her the photo, only to find that she was distracted, chatting up some American boy.

Now, I turn back to apologize for that, but — again — she is not with me. She is walking down a stone stairway toward the riverbank. I follow.

She's heading toward a kiosk selling tickets for the tour boats that crawl up and down the Seine. She stops at the bottom of the steps, pointing to them as I draw up alongside her. "Do you have to prebook these boat tours, or can you just buy tickets on the day of?" she asks.

"If they are not full, you can get on," I tell her, as she pulls out that crumpled ball of paper from her bag. It looks like it belongs in the trash can. ("Trash can"? *Mon dieu*, I'm starting to think American, too!) She smooths it out, looks from it to the board outside the kiosk and back again. Puts the paper in front of my face.

"Do these boats go to all these places?"

I quickly check. "Most of them."

She gives a happy gasp. "So, if we take one of these boats, we can cross off lots of the sights I had planned ..."

I look at the river, then at the wall of gray hanging over the water. It's as if a great chunk of the cloudy sky has fallen to the earth. How much is she going to see? But she's walking to the kiosk now, so ... I guess I'm going on a boat tour.

Inside, she greets the clerk behind the counter. "*Bonjourno!* Wait, no — that's Italian. I mean, *Bonjour!*" I see her embarrassed expression reflected in the glass, superimposed on the clerk's scowl. Is she scowling because of Serena's mistake, or because of the Santa hat and reindeer sweater she's wearing? I'm guessing this outfit was not her choice, but her manager's. Probably catering to tourists, from America or England, trying to make them feel a bit more at home at Christmas.

Because she has exhausted what French she has, Serena holds up two fingers and says "Tickets" while trying to drag her accent over the Atlantic. The price flashes up on the digital display over the cash register, and Serena hands over some euros. I'm about to repeat my earlier question, will she really get to *experience* Paris from a boat? And does she have X-ray glasses that will allow her to see through the fog? But the way she's thanking the clerk as she takes the tickets strikes me as pure and honest. I take another photograph of her eager expression: she's excited just to be here. Plus, there will be lots of *people* on board, which will surely satisfy Monsieur Deschamps, so maybe this *isn't* the worst thing that could have happened.

Serena turns away from the booth, putting the tickets into her bag as we head back outside. "Well," she says, "we now know what we're doing at three thirty! We *just* missed the two thirty, apparently."

I check my watch, see that we have fifty-seven minutes to kill. I'm about to ask Serena what she wants to do, but — from the way she is looking at me — I can tell that she has an idea.

"Can we *please* go to Shakespeare and Company now?"

*

"I gotta say ..." Serena laughs as we walk past the bistro on rue de la Bûcherie. "I sort of admire your country's commitment to smoking."

She gestures to the patrons dining on the sidewalk, some of their faces lit a lurid red by the glow of the heater lamps placed outside. Row after row of them — empty plates on the table, half-full wineglasses in one hand, cigarettes in the other. I want to take a photo, but their very serious looks are kind of intimidating, in a very "French" way — even to me.

We pass the bistro and come upon the dark green façade of Shakespeare and Company. Serena stops to take a picture on her phone.

"This place is about a hundred years old, right?" she asks.

"Yes and no," I say, as we go inside. It is pleasantly warm, compared to the street, but the first blast of the musty old book smell always makes my stomach flip. "The original Shakespeare and Company was over in the 6th arrondissement, but it was forced to close when France was occupied during the Second World War. This store opened after the war, in the fifties. I believe it was first called something else but later changed its name. In tribute, I think."

I have always had a soft spot for this place. I know some people chafe at its cramped layout and find the way you constantly bump into strangers quite irritating. But to me, this is a fair trade for the silence inside. It's so peaceful — more like a library than a store.

Until Serena goes stomping through the store in her orange sneakers. I follow her. "Are you looking for something in particular?" I ask. She nods. "Was there not a bookstore at the airport?"

"I have to get it *here*."

We walk up the stairs to the first floor, and I have to press myself against one wall to allow a middle-aged couple to pass me on their way down. When we get up there, Serena goes straight to the poetry section, which lines three of the four walls around the landing.

I leave her to it, drifting over to the only wall not lined with books. Instead, there is a noticeboard covered in scraps of paper, cards and Post-it notes. A small tray with a sign that says — in English — "Lonely Hearts and Missed Connections." A few Sharpies and pencils, some Scotch tape and thumbtacks, for anyone who wants to ... what? Profess their love to nobody? Let store patrons know how much their hearts are hurting?

I take a step closer, skimming the notes. They are pinned chaotically, occasionally on top of each other — sentiments fighting for space.

Christina: My education began too late ...

My heart is punctured, Mary ...

Danielle: Your smile saved my life ...

There's even a whole poem, and when I see a line that says, "I now try not to think of you, lest I drain the well of my memory," I check that no one is looking at me, and that my camera's flash is off — because Shakespeare and Company has many signs saying "No Photos" — then steal a few shots of the whole board. I want to read through it later.

I turn back to Serena, when suddenly I *feel* the wall and the noticeboard behind me. I am remembering one of the last times I was here, with Martine, how she spent at least half an hour reading note after note. We had each other at the time, so I couldn't understand why she seemed so keen to take a walk in other people's sad shoes, but she told me she found it enchanting: "Just so romantic ..."

I wonder if she might have returned here after our breakup and left a note of her own. A note for me.

I don't trust myself not to look, so I tell Serena I am going downstairs to browse.

*

After I've looked through the philosophy section, I turn to go back up, only to see Serena on the ground floor, too, thanking the sales clerk for something. I assume she's asking after whatever book it is she came here to find. When she returns to the poetry section, I follow.

She reaches up to the top shelf to move books aside, cursing out loud at the cloud of dust that settles on her face. She grimaces, coughs … then she goes back to scanning the titles, actually getting down on her hands and knees, slowly crawling backward, her face very close to the spines.

"You were looking at the H–J books before," I say. "Now, you are in the Ts … Do you not know the author?"

"Yes, I do, but sometimes people are assholes."

What do the two have to do with each other? "I do not understand."

She crawls backward two steps, looking again at books she's already passed. I hope she is being careful — she came very close to falling down the stairs just now. "Sometimes people put books back in the wrong place," she explains. "So, I'm just making *extra-*sure it isn't here."

"Making sure *what* isn't here?"

She sighs, straightening up and sitting back on her heels. Her hair has started to come loose, arcing off at the sides like exploding fireworks. "*Death of a Naturalist* by Seamus Heaney. I was hoping this store would have a copy."

"You cannot get this book in New York?"

"Probably, but ... getting it from here would have been more special."

"Why is that?"

She starts to answer, but then my eyes stray to a clock on the wall. It is 3:25 p.m. ...

"The boat!" I blurt out. "We only have five minutes before it leaves."

"Damn it ..." She scrambles to her feet, and we hurry back outside. After the warmth of the bookstore, the Christmas chill is like a giant knife, scraping at my skin. I turn up the collar of my jacket, then take Serena's hand and lead her off in a run.

It's only after we've turned the corner onto Quai de Montebello that I realize we're holding hands.

And there is not a tour boat in sight. I check my watch and see that it is now 3:32 p.m. The dock is empty, and even though the boat can't have gone far in two minutes, the veil of fog looks to have swallowed it already. I'm almost outraged that it left on time. Serena's grip on my hand tightens, but I can't bring myself to look at her. I don't want to see her disappointment.

When I finally steal a glance, she is staring out at the Seine, tears like sparkling crystals in her eyes. My fingers twitch, and I wrestle with the urge to reach for my camera again. As beautiful as the moment is, I know I would be crossing a line by gathering up all of her sadness for myself.

"I am sorry that we missed the boat," I tell her.

She looks at the ground, sniffles. "It's not just that ... I'm upset about not finding the book."

"But you said you would be able to find it in New York."

She lets her bag drop to the floor, runs her hands through her hair. Makes it wilder, if that is possible. "That's not the point. It was my dad's favorite book of poetry, and he told me once that, when he saw this old, beat-up edition in Shakespeare and Company, he couldn't not buy it for Mom. And Mom always told me, she didn't really get the poems in it, but she loved it anyway, because it meant so much to Dad ..." Her voice cracks, and I see her clench her teeth, trying not to cry. "It's a special book. I don't know how it happened, but ... a few years ago, Mom realized she had lost it. I thought, if I could replace it for her ..."

I give her time to speak, but she just shakes her head as if there is no second half to that sentence.

"Maybe your mother would not want it replaced," I say. "It may look the same, but a new book won't have old memories ... Your father already gave her those."

Serena looks at me, her eyes frozen as though she doesn't understand what I've said. After a moment, she starts to nod in agreement — but she only gets halfway through the motion when she starts to cry. I guide her to a bench and sit her down, then turn and scurry back to where she left her bag. I put it between us as I sit beside her on the bench.

"My dad died," she blurts out. She seems almost shocked, and I wonder if it's her first time saying the words out loud. "Lara probably told you this already but — two years ago — he went out to work and never came home. Car wreck ... That's why I'm on this trip. It was supposed to be a way for us all to remember him ... Because that's what's been bothering me all these years, you know? That one day, a man who I saw every day of my life could just *not be there* anymore. Like he never existed."

"But he did exist," I tell her. "You remember him."

"That's just it. I think I'm ... actually starting to forget. You know, sometimes I have to really concentrate, just to remember his face. Like when I try, this ... this" — she jabs a finger toward the river — "fog just fills my head and I can't quite see him. My own dad ... He's almost like a ghost in my mind at this point. A ghost that's disappearing. How can that be fair? That such a big presence in your life eventually becomes just a wisp of memory?"

"It isn't fair," I agree. There must be something in my voice that gives me away, because the look on her face tells me she knows there is more I am not saying. "I have not lost a parent, but ... my grandpapa, he, ah ... he has Alzheimer's. He helped raise me after me and Mama returned to France, but now he doesn't recognize me ... doesn't recognize any of the people around him. He lives with my mother but thinks she's his sister, and when I go home to visit, he thinks I'm just some kid they've hired to clean the house. Those days are tough. A few years ago, when we noticed the first signs, we would correct him — tell him, 'No, Delphine is your daughter, not your sister. Jean-Luc is your grandson.' But now it upsets him too much to try to figure it all out, and so ... we just go along with it."

Serena looks at me, her eyes shining. "So, you know?"

You know. She does not have to say what. "I know."

"And he doesn't remember you at all?"

"Sometimes he does." My eyes begin to prickle, and my throat feels like I've just tried to swallow a tennis ball.

I look at my feet, wondering why I am about to tell a girl I met just today something I never even told Martine. "Sometimes, he will look at old photos, and if I'm next to him, and he sees a picture of the two of us, he will point at me, and I can tell that he knows who I am, for just a moment. But that's all it is — a moment ..."

"A wisp."

I nod. "But my grandpapa, he cannot hold on to his memories." I look back up at her. "Whatever you must do to hold on to *your* memories, you should do it." Now I understand a little more about her scrapbook.

Serena leans across the bench and hugs me, tight. Wild tendrils of her hair jab into my eyes. It's a strange feeling, getting this burst of affection from someone who has seemed irritated by me many times today. But I guess we could both do with a hug.

Just as I'm lifting my hands to hug her back, though, I see something over her shoulder.

"Serena," I whisper. "I think that's our boat!"

~ CHAPTER SEVEN ~
SERENA

3:39 P.M.

I extract myself from Jean-Luc and turn back to the river. He's right: a boat — long and sleek, with tinted windows — is slowly docking, the fog lifting from it. On the dock is a harassed-looking twenty-something guy in a black shirt and pants, with a clipboard, welcoming a few people who are waiting to get on. The boat looks even swankier than I expected.

We head over and join the small group boarding. I notice one of them — a short, squat guy with severe sideburns and a very haughty face — kind of pause when he sees me, his eyes going right to my orange sneakers. Why? Just because he is dressed to the nines just for a tour. In fact, his whole group looks like they're going for dinner at a five-star restaurant.

But this is Paris, the world capital of fashion …

When it's our turn to speak to Monsieur Clipboard — whose

shirt is also fancy, except for the hummingbird on it — I start to dig out my tickets from my bag, but he just waves us on — I guess, to save some time. Part of me thinks I totally wasted twenty-two euros. A bigger part of me is like, *Yeah, sure, Serena — like you'd ever have the nerve to con your way onto a tour boat.*

"Let's find a spot with a good view," I tell Jean-Luc.

"A good view of *what*?" he asks, gesturing at the interior of the boat. He's got a point — whereas the boats docked near the ticket booth had bench seats lining the windows, this one just has an empty floor, with a few small tables by the walls. The space is a lake of black and chrome. Certainly stylish but definitely not seasonal. Inside the doorway is an actual bar, and the speakers in the corners are playing jazz so smooth that I almost want to cough at the smoke I'm imagining filling the room.

"Maybe I got tickets to the party boat and didn't notice?" I say.

Jean-Luc just laughs as we walk in. We hand our coats and bags off to another guy wearing a hummingbird shirt and sit down at a table. I can't tell if it's the tinted windows or just the fog or the weird lights in here — but the view of Paris is not exactly stunning. It feels more like I'm viewing it through polluted water.

Beside me, Jean-Luc shifts as he reaches into his pocket for his vibrating cell phone. From the way he stares at the screen (and the "+1" telephone code), I gather that "Paul Thayer" is his dad.

Jean-Luc rejects the call. Sees me looking at him. Shrugs. "Just my father, probably calling to ask if I have an answer."

"An answer to what?"

He puts his phone back in his jeans pocket. "He's inviting me to stay with him in the summer."

"That's nice of him." From Jean-Luc's grimace, I assume this was the wrong thing for me to say. But before I can follow up, a French voice startles me.

"*Madame, Monsieur?*" Yet another guy in a hummingbird shirt is looming over us, holding a tray of what looks like champagne.

I start to raise a hand in refusal, then remember — this is Europe, so I'm of legal drinking age. I take a flute, then look to Jean-Luc. "Is this how it's done in Paris? Champagne for showing up?"

He shrugs back as he takes his own glass. "A special treat for Christmas?"

Of course the tour company would want to make the most of the festive season. Pretty cool that the drinks are free — I just wish I could see the sights of Paris a little better, but maybe the lights in here will go down once we set off?

I start to take a sip, but the boat lurches away from the dock, and I miss my mouth. I reach into my pocket for a tissue, laughing at myself. "Classy," I tell Jean-Luc.

But he's not listening to me. He's eavesdropping on the well-dressed couple standing near us. As the jazz song slowly fades, I catch a snippet of French. I don't understand a word, but the tone is definitely flirtatious.

I nudge Jean-Luc. "You know, it's not nice to listen in on a private conversation."

His eyebrows knit together, almost like *he's* unable to understand them — which, of course, can't be right.

"No, it's not that," he says. "I'm just surprised that I'm hearing only French people." He leans back on the bench, his eyes sweeping the room, which lightly dips and rises with the swells of the Seine. "Where are all the Americans in baseball caps?"

Now that he's mentioned it, I start to wonder, too. At first, I just have a mild feeling something's off — but then a guy in a sharp suit walks by and gives us a kind of stink eye, and my gut starts to churn a little bit. It can't just be my orange sneakers — something is *way* off here.

"Um, are you sure this is actually a tour boat?"

Jean-Luc doesn't get a chance to answer, because a pinstriped arm appears out of nowhere and a perfectly manicured hand lifts him by the elbow to his feet. The rest of the man appears like he's being drawn rapidly by an invisible artist. He's a heavy guy, whose flushed cheeks tell me that he's gone to town on the free bubbly. He starts talking in rapid French. It sounds like he's asking a question, and Jean-Luc is … nodding? It's hard to tell. He looks hesitant for a second, before he relaxes and begins to speak freely. The only word I make out is *"Américaine,"* and that might only be because he points at me when he says it.

Mr. Pinstripe turns to me and extends his hand, as a saxophone cover of a famous song, the title of which escapes me, starts up. His hand is clammy and gross, and his face is very serious as he practically bellows over the music: *"Allô!"*

"Hi!" I shout back, shooting a look at Jean-Luc in the hope that his expression might explain what's going on here. His eyes tell me that, whatever is going on, it's *bad …*

Mr. Pinstripe hollers again and leaves us, gesturing to the bar in the center of the room and spreading his hands as if to say, "Everything's free."

Now Jean-Luc takes my hand and guides me to the bar. I'm

painfully self-conscious of the clamminess I caught from Mr. Pinstripe, but Jean-Luc doesn't seem to care. He finishes his champagne, then signals an order to the bartender. He looks left and right, as if making sure we won't be overheard.

When he confirms we're in the clear, he leans in so close his lips brush the top of my ear. It's the kind of thing I would *usually* find a little gross. "I have good news and bad news," he says. "Which would you like to hear first?"

He leans back so I have to lean forward and shout into his ear. This conversation better be short, otherwise there's a good chance we'll both leave this boat deaf! "Does anyone *ever* ask for the good news first? Give me the bad."

"The bad news is that this is not a tour boat. It is a boat hired out by some company called Colibri. That is French for 'humming-bird.'" *Aha.* "This is their Christmas soirée."

I put my face in my hands. "Oh, God, that's what that big guy came over for? Is he going to throw us overboard for gate-crashing?"

When I look back up at him, he is grinning and blushing. "Well, this is the thing ... Apparently, I look like someone they have just hired to start in the new year. An accountant named Louis. So ... we have gotten away with it. For now."

The bartender — a tall, pale woman with her hair pulled back into a topknot so tight that I worry it might pull the skin off her face — comes over with a couple more flutes of champagne. Jean-Luc thanks her.

"It is not all bad," he says, raising a glass in a toast. "Louis from Accounting drinks for free."

"And who do they think *I* am?"

He pauses, mid-sip. From the way he's blushing again, I get the feeling I'm not going to like the answer. "Ah, well, I was thinking quickly, and I figured that maybe Louis would have a — how you say? — plus one. So I tell him … that you are my girlfriend from America."

Well, I don't know what to say to *that*.

Then something else — something a bit more *relevant* — hits me. "Hey … where exactly is this boat going?"

He just shrugs at me. "It will probably travel along the Seine for a while, then turn around and come back."

"What about the Romance Tour?" This time, when I shout in his ear, I might be *trying* to give him a bit of an earache. Just a little.

Jean-Luc pats the air in a *calm down* sort of gesture. "If we try to get off now, we will have to get them to stop the boat and turn back. We will be ruining their whole party. I don't see what other choice we have. We're not getting off unless there's some kind of emergency. I don't suppose you have any heart condition?"

"I feel like I'm getting one," I tell him.

He doesn't say anything. He just slides the other flute toward me, raising his eyebrows. "Hey, we're here … might as well try to enjoy it, huh?"

I pick up the champagne glass and look away. Of course *he* doesn't think it's a big deal to be crashing a party in Paris — people who live here tend not to have one-day itineraries burning holes in their coat pockets.

Then the smooth jazz explodes into "Get Lucky" by Daft Punk, and a roar goes up from the Hummingbird crew. I don't know if it's because they really like the song or because the elevator music has gone away. Even though my mind is furious about yet another diversion, my body (well, my head and my shoulders) totally sells me out. This song challenges anyone not to dance.

"You like this song?"

I dodge the question by throwing back my champagne. I look away from Jean-Luc again — not to hide my embarrassment, but because chugging the champagne just made me erupt into a huge sneeze. When I turn back to Jean-Luc, he is standing very formally, offering me a handshake. A handshake? No: he's asking me to dance.

I let him lead me onto the dance floor — which is jam-packed with French office types — thinking, Jean-Luc is right, there's really not much that we can do about our current situation. I bet Mom and Dad hit a few stumbling blocks on their honeymoon, right? They would also want me to have some fun. *And I do love this song ...*

*

4·33 P.M.

When the waiter passes by with a tray of champagne, I turn him down because I'm still in the middle of trying (failing) to do the cha-cha. We've been here about an hour, and I've just finished my third drink. If I have a fourth, I might not remember the awesome time I'm surprised I'm having at a floating office party with a crowd of French strangers.

When the song comes to a close, I look around for Jean-Luc. He's standing on a chair — taking photos of the party. He's got a big grin on his face, and it makes me happy to see this.

Then I wonder why the music hasn't come back on.

Everyone falls silent and looks toward the far corner of the room. A spotlight — there's a spotlight? How did I *ever* mistake this for a tour boat? — falls on a small raised stage, where Mr. Pinstripe has a microphone. He says a few things in French and gets a cheer. He says something else in French and gets a boo. A big, huge laugh for the next thing in French, and my champagne buzz is starting to fade. I start looking for the waiter. *Actually, a fourth drink sounds like an excellent idea now …*

"… Louis!"

Uh-oh. I don't need to speak French to know who Mr. Pinstripe is talking to. The spotlight almost blinds me as it searches for Jean-Luc — still standing on a chair and unable to escape the attention of his "colleagues," who start chanting: "Lou-is! Lou-is! Lou-is!"

Jean-Luc clambers down from the chair, looking like he wants to crawl into the nearest hole or just dive overboard. I weave my way through a few bodies to get to him.

"What's going on?" I ask.

"Apparently, *Louis* is a good singer," he whispers to me. "With a voice like Johnny Hallyday."

"Who?" I ask, but Jean-Luc just waves his hand, like, *Forget it.* I can see his sweaty forehead glistening under the spotlight. It literally follows him wherever he moves. "Louis's colleagues at the Bordeaux branch 'always talk about his amazing voice …'"

That's when the horrible truth hits me. "They're asking you to *sing*?"

"Unfortunately." He looks past me, then left and then right.

"*Can* you sing?" I ask.

"Absolutely not," he says, suddenly pasting on a smile and nodding at someone.

"What do we do?" I ask.

"Abandon ship?"

But even as we're whispering back and forth, the crowd is pushing us toward the stage. Either he fesses up to *not* being Louis from Accounting, or he gets up on stage and prays his voice sounds like Johnny Hallyday — whoever that is.

The way the crowd parts for "Louis" as he makes his way to the stage would be really impressive if Jean-Luc's shoulders weren't slumped like he's on his way to the electric chair. He smiles at Mr. Pinstripe, nods, takes the microphone from him and mumbles something in French. I see him gesture to his throat and assume he's trying to con them with a story about being under the weather. Pretty smart, although all his "colleagues" groan in disappointment.

I catch Jean-Luc's eye and give him a sly thumbs-up, like, *Good thinking.* He's totally got this.

He smiles, then goes back to chatting up the crowd. Blah-blah-French-blah-blah, "*d'Amérique ...*"

Huh ... That sure sounded like "America." What is he —

"Serena!"

He points, and the spotlight comes for me, too. Now he's gesturing me up to the stage, and the French people are applauding like I've just won an award, and my legs are walking me over there, and I'm accepting the microphone he's handing to me, even though my head is screaming: *What the hell is going on!?*

I place my hand over the microphone and ask Jean-Luc exactly that.

"I said I am not feeling well," he mumbles, "and that I need my American girlfriend to duet with me. Do you know 'O Holy Night'?"

"Sort of. In *English*," I hiss.

"It's okay — no one expects you to be bilingual."

I turn my back to the crowd so no one can see *just* how much I'm freaking out "'O Holy Night,' though? Seriously?"

"What's wrong with that?"

"Well …" I glance back over my shoulder, at the very sophisticated French office crowd. "It's kind of impossible to sing."

The smile he gives me looks like it's about twenty percent humor and eighty percent absolute terror. "With our combined talents, does it matter?"

Then he signals to the DJ to start, and the music kicks in, and I take a deep breath. I guess I'm going for it. Today has already been a disaster. What's the worst that can happen now?

*

4:48 P.M.

The worst that could happen is that my average singing and Jean-Luc's apparently abysmal Johnny Hallyday impression get us chucked overboard. (That doesn't happen.)

The *second worst* thing that could happen is that the French people revolt, pelting us with canapés and champagne, while we wait for the boat to dock so that we can be kicked off. (That doesn't happen, either.)

What actually happens is probably the third worst thing. Jean-Luc sings, and he sounds ... well, not terrible, but not great — and I'm guessing nothing like Johnny Hallyday — and everyone realizes that he's not Louis from Accounting, new in from Bordeaux. Our duet is greeted with a stony silence — which, I've got to be honest, bums me out, because I felt like *I* wasn't all that bad! It's been years since I have been on a stage, and this was *a lot* better than the time I sang "Defying Gravity" with my friend Ariana, in our high school senior year. (The less said about *that* ...) There's something joyful about singing — even if you're not a great singer, it still feels good to be "loud."

But now Mr. Pinstripe is pulling Jean-Luc aside to have a conversation with him. I look down at the floor so that I don't make eye contact with anyone, and then Mr. Pinstripe storms off, his face tomato-red, and I assume he's going to talk with the captain about the stowaways. A few minutes after *that*, the boat suddenly lurches to the right, like it's docking.

Jean-Luc and I retreat into the corner as half the partygoers continue glaring at us. The other half turns away and tries to forget all about us. I look at Jean-Luc, who's looking at his shoes.

The waiter appears with our coats and bags, and the boat is slowing down, and I'm in a bit of a pickle because, after all that champagne, I kind of really need to pee, but I'm too embarrassed to speak up and ask where the bathroom is.

Finally, the boat stops, and Mr. Pinstripe says something sharp. I don't need to speak French to know that he's asking (ordering) us to get the hell off his boat! I follow Jean-Luc to the exit, searching for the French word for "sorry," but all I can think to say is, *"Pardon, pardon, pardon."* Mr. Pinstripe actually blocks my way and points to the microphone that I forgot I was still holding. *Oh, right.* Somehow, handing it back to him is the worst part of this whole humiliation.

About a minute later, I'm back on the street, shrugging on my parka, hooking my cross-body bag over my shoulder, and it's only *after* I've done it that I realize it might be odd for me to take Jean-Luc's arm and press myself to him for warmth. But it's late December in Paris, and I'm pretty sure even the average penguin would be like, "Are you kidding me with this?"

I let him go when he comes to a dead stop. Guess he's not keen on an almost-stranger overstepping boundaries.

Then I see that his expression isn't uncomfortable. His eyes are darting all over the place, and his jaw is a little clenched.

"What's wrong?" I ask him. "I mean, besides the obvious." He gives the one answer I absolutely do not want to hear right now.

"I have no idea where we are."

CHAPTER EIGHT

JEAN-LUC

17H40

"Is she your girlfriend?"

Monsieur Zidane is grinning at us from behind the counter of his shoebox of a café, which we ducked into because Serena needed to use the bathroom. He introduced himself immediately and began brewing the coffees we ordered, with a smile like he'd been waiting all day for us to come in. He looks like he might have been handsome in the seventies, but now his cheeks are jowly and his bushy eyebrows seem to be reaching for the opposite wall — the whole effect makes my skin crawl a little. I'm glad Serena doesn't speak French.

"What's he saying?" she asks, in between sips of her take-out latte, which she then holds up to her chin for warmth as we shift toward the door …

I can't think of a good lie, nor a reasonable explanation for why

I very quickly shake my head at the old man behind the counter. So I simply wave him away and answer in French: "We're just friends."

He calls me a fool and says that I should change that as quickly as possible. I try not to blush nor to launch into an explanation of the madness of this day — how bereavement, stress, mistaken identity and getting thrown off a boat are not exactly good setups for romance. Not that I'm saying that is what I am after, of course.

Once Serena and I are outside, I look up and down the street, starting to breathe a little easier for the first time since we were ejected from the party boat. For all my worrying before, it took only a quick glance at my phone and ten minutes of walking to get us back to somewhat familiar territory. Not a neighborhood I know *that* well, but we're back within the *Périph*, the ring road that forms the unofficial boundary of the city — I'm pretty sure I'm going to see something I recognize pretty soon, and I won't have to worry about looking lost in front of Serena.

I don't know why the thought of that bothers me *quite* so much.

When I see headlights coming toward us, I think that our run of bad luck — getting on the wrong boat, slaughtering a Christmas carol, getting thrown off outside the *Périph*, then a mad dash through a bad neighborhood, looking for a café so that Serena could use the bathroom — is coming to an end with a taxi appearing out of nowhere to save us.

But — *merde!* — it's just an ordinary car.

A flash of white appears in the corner of my eye. Serena is beside me at the curb, holding her coffee in one hand and her itinerary in the other. With a huff, she stuffs it back into her cross-body bag. "I don't even know why I'm still bothering to look at this thing. The Romance Tour is an unmitigated failure."

To be honest, I prefer her pronouncing it ruined than constantly fretting over what she will and will not be able to see, which is what she was doing after we left the pier, right when I was trying not to look too anxious.

We fall into another silence as we walk and drink our coffees. Monsieur Zidane might have been a little bit creepy in how he, apparently, seemed really keen that I ask Serena out — if that's what he meant with those raised eyebrows — but I have to give him some credit: his espresso is very good.

If I'm remembering correctly, we have to take the next right, which I *think* is the road that leads us to Parc Sainte-Périne. I am about to tell Serena that we will turn off soon, when I hear her sigh heavily.

"I can't believe how much of a disaster this has been," she says. "My mom's not here, my sister is off with her latest BF" — I think she means "boyfriend" — "and I've barely taken *any* photos for the scrapbook I'm supposed to be putting together for us. All I've got are a couple of street shots and a picture of *you*. Like, how am I supposed to give that as a gift? 'Sorry, Mom, I didn't make it to the Eiffel Tower, but here — have a candid of a French boy who doesn't even know the words to "O Holy Night"!'"

"Look, please be quiet!" I snap at her. "I cannot get us out of here if you keep complaining to me about everything. So, please, calm down and stay quiet so I can figure out where we go now!" I say this even though I think I've pretty much figured out where we need to go — I kind of just want her to stop talking, just for a while.

Then I feel her annoyance, sense that she's staring daggers at the back of my head. I suppose I *was* out of line for raising my voice. I know by now the fact that she had important plans for today is probably both sad and comical to her. But *I* had plans today, too. I've been running around with her for almost eight hours at this point, and I'll be shocked if I have taken more than three or four usable shots for my project. There are certainly lots of *people* in the photos I took on the party boat, but that's all that was — a party on a boat. I don't think Monsieur Deschamps will really accept that as a theme. I might actually end up failing. While Serena is trying to grab hold of her parents' past, I feel like I am watching my future drift away from me.

She huffs again. "Whose bright idea was it to get on that boat anyway?"

I turn around so quickly that she almost walks right into me. "*Yours!* It was you who bought tickets for the boat tour!" I'm yelling at her again, and I feel a flush of shame in my chest, because I'm not the type of person who yells this much — but whether it's her or this crazy day, I find myself yelling at this American girl quite a lot.

It's only when I see Serena roll her eyes that I know: a) she's not going to get upset at being yelled at, and b) she's about to yell at me, just as loudly.

"Yes, a boat *tour*," she says, "which was *not* what that was. But who was it at the pier, who said, 'Seh-ree-*nah*, I fink zattz aur *bott*'?" (Is that really how I sound?)

I start to throw my hands in the air, then remember that I'm holding a coffee, which I'd rather not send flying. "I would not have made this mistake," I tell her, "if I had not been so focused on trying to cheer *you* up."

"And why are you even bothering to do that? You were just supposed to open the door, give me a key and let me crash in your dorm for one night — why are you acting like I'm somehow your responsibility?"

"Because I was starting to like being with you."

I feel as surprised as Serena looks by what I've just said, but I realize it's true — it's been quite a while since I've mentally cursed out Henri for saddling me with a guest. A good few hours since I've wondered if we should maybe go our separate ways. All of a sudden, the very talkative Serena seems not to know what to say. I'd be relieved at having a break from being yelled at, were it not for how *awkward* this moment feels. My eyes go to the sidewalk, and it takes a lot of effort to lift them so that I can look at her. Her mouth opens as if she wants to say something, but she doesn't — she just freezes, her eyes narrowing like I have spoken in French and she's trying to figure out what I said.

I can still see her absurd orange shoes on the upper edge of my vision, and she starts to step toward me. At first, I wonder what she's doing — is she going to give me a hug? Or is she going to punch me for talking to her the way I have?

"Taxi! Taxi!" She tugs on my sleeve to make me look up. "What's the French for 'taxi'?"

"'Taxi,'" I tell her, turning around and seeing a taxi crawling toward us, its headlights looking a bit nightmarish as they pierce the thick fog. I'm so grateful to have the awkward moment interrupted, I practically throw myself in front of it to flag it down. The driver — whose craggy, pockmarked face looks like it might crumble if he smiled — gives us a dirty look but beckons us in.

As we get in the back, I notice that there's an unopened Christmas present on the front passenger seat. It's poorly wrapped, so I figure it's something the driver is planning to give to someone. I wonder if it's for a partner or maybe his child?

"*Merci, merci ...*" Serena pulls out her itinerary again, squints at it and then leans forward, saying, "Um ... Maison d'angle? Bistro. Montmartre?"

A restaurant? I was not expecting that. I assumed we were headed to the Arc de Triomphe or Sacré-Cœur or some other tourist mob scene. But the driver nods like he knows the place. It sounds familiar to me, too, but I can't think why. I'm too busy looking at the dashboard clock, which hasn't even ticked to six p.m. yet — Americans eat dinner so *early*!

✱

The drive into Montmartre takes almost twenty minutes because of traffic, and Serena and I are silent throughout. Partly because we carried our awkward silence into the taxi, but also because Serena is writing a new itinerary down on a fresh piece of paper. I hear her sigh every now and then.

I am not exactly in the best of moods myself as the taxi climbs the steep roads up into Montmartre. Out the window, I see nothing but a foggy night, the weak glow of streetlights looking like fire under water. The conditions today have been totally against me. Even if we had not been stuck on the party boat during sunset — magical natural light that makes even amateurs look like they have a good eye — there would have been no chance of me finding inspiration in the city. I had fun shooting the party, but I'm not going to impress Monsieur Deschamps with a series of photos of drunk office types dabbing … badly.

Perhaps I *should* have left Serena to it. After all, she had her itinerary and her phone — she probably wouldn't have gotten lost, even if she'd been by herself. And I wouldn't be the fool hoping to "stumble" into inspiration, so close to his deadline …

Now we've hit traffic on Boulevard de Clichy. I don't know how long we go without moving in terms of minutes and seconds, but the red digits on the dashboard tell me that we sit still for two euros and thirty cents. The taxi fare to Montmartre is going to take a greedy bite out of the cash in my wallet.

When the fare goes up another twenty cents while we're still not moving, Serena leans forward and taps on the screen dividing the driver from his passengers. With big gestures, she indicates that she would like him to let us out, then she shoves some euros at him. She thanks him (in English), then climbs out of the taxi. I get out the other side, running around the trunk and weaving my way through the bumpers of the creeping cars, to join her on the sidewalk.

"I had to get out of that cab," she huffs, running a hand through her wild curls. She pushes her itinerary at me and taps an address. "Do you know if it's far? Maison d'angle?"

"Just up rue Lepic, then turn right on Abbesses," I tell her, still wondering why this bistro sounds familiar to me.

"Cool," she mumbles, her whole face bathed in the lurid red glow of the Moulin Rouge as we sidestep a crowd of tourists taking photos on their phones. I stay one step ahead of Serena, trying to block her view of the … gentleman's club that is opposite the famous venue, but I know she's seen it when I hear her laugh.

"You are offended?" I ask her.

"What? Do you think I've never walked past a strip club before? I'm from New York."

We walk in silence up rue Lepic, beneath the starry string lights that crisscross the street for Christmas. Serena seems befuddled that burlesque clubs stand so casually among ordinary businesses, like convenience stores, and butchers' shops. I see her cover her nose at the strong scents wafting off the rotisseries that turn slowly, almost sadistically, out on the sidewalk.

We turn off Lepic onto Abbesses, which has nicer restaurants and some decent bars, but they still compete with cheap grocers for business.

I look to Serena and see that her eyes are wide as she takes it all in. It's not a "pretty" part of Paris, but I guess it's still striking to a visitor. The photography student in me really wishes he could see Paris anew, the way she's doing; wishes he could borrow her eyes …

I'm not going to say this to her, though. I have a feeling she'll take it literally!

Then we come to a stop outside a large restaurant on a corner. Maison d'angle — The Corner House. I wonder again why its name sounds familiar. I certainly haven't eaten here before. I see Serena in profile. Her cheeks are a little flushed, lashed by the winter wind, and the line of her jaw is set firm and tight. She is staring at the bistro, determined and exhausted all at once. From the way her eyes widen, and the corner of her mouth begins to lift in a smile, I can tell that this is one of the more meaningful stops on her itinerary.

"Your parents ate here?" I ask.

She nods, doesn't take her eyes off the door: "Yeah. Dad said they got lunch here once — they had a reservation at some super-fancy restaurant, but Mom left the directions at the hotel, and they couldn't find it. Plus, it was twenty-five years ago, so they couldn't look it up on their phones or anything like that. So they were walking around, and it started to rain — they literally just walked into the first place that they passed ... *This* place. Maison d'angle. They were wet and tired and lost, but Dad said they had an amazing meal, and that it was at *that* moment, he knew their new marriage would last forever. Because ..." Her voice catches, and I hear her take a deep, steadying breath. "Because everything 'just had a way of working out for the best.'"

My heart quickens at the puff of misty breath escaping her lips. It looks like a tiny rain cloud, a rain cloud looming over her heart.

"Man, this is so weird," she says, her voice so low I'm not even sure she's talking to *me* at first. "I'm in another country, but I feel like I'm closer to my dad, somehow. Maybe because I'm standing somewhere he once stood."

My hands move without me thinking about it — I take her photo again. But Serena does not react to that — she smiles at the wonder of this moment, of really walking in her parents' foot-steps, before walking up to the door, taking the stone steps two at a time. She tries the handle but finds it locked. She turns and looks at me. "It's closed ... damn it!"

"We are early," I explain.

"But it's after six."

"Six o'clock is not dinnertime in Paris."

"Well, *that's* ridiculous ..." She leans right up against the glass, to peer inside. "You're telling me the French don't *ever* get hungry before seven?"

Because this place is meaningful to her, I choose not to rise to this taunt.

Serena startles and jumps back when a man appears behind the glass. He's dressed all in black, with a hairstyle so puffy and rounded, it looks like a pancake on his head — a *bouffant* if ever I saw it. His name badge says "Didier." He gestures at us to go away, but Serena clasps her hands together and makes a face so pleading, he opens the door.

Serena starts talking before he can say anything. "Excuse me, sir, but what time do you open?"

"Six thirty. You come back then." Didier's English is good, but his accent is *torturing* the vowels.

Serena makes a sound that is caught between a gasp and a sigh. "Listen, I know I might be out of line here, but I've had a really crappy day" — I bristle at that — "and it would be really great if I could get out of the cold for a little bit. Is there, like, any chance we could just come inside and have a drink while we wait for the kitchen to open?"

Didier thinks about it for a second, then nods. "I suppose it will be okay for you to come in and have a drink," he says. Then he takes a step back and holds the door all the way open. "After all, it is almost Christmas."

"Oh, thank you, sir!" Serena takes a hold of my sleeve and drags me in after her. "You are very, very kind, thank you!"

We follow Didier through the restaurant. It looks kind of eerie without people. I can't stop myself imagining that there *were* people here just before we arrived, but they came to a bad end — and Didier is now leading us into a trap.

On instinct, I ask him if we might sit at a small table in the far corner, because I will feel better if I can see the whole room. He just shrugs as if to say, *Whatever,* and we sit down. Serena picks up a drink menu and turns it over in her hand, quickly reading and asking for a Coke. After all the champagne on board the party boat, I guess she does not need any more alcohol. I ask for the same. Didier disappears to fetch them, leaving us alone.

I feel instantly uncomfortable with the silence. After a few moments of awkward fidgeting, I lean toward Serena and say, "I am sorry … for yelling at you earlier. I was tired — but that is no excuse, I should not have been so hard on you."

She smiles at me. "I don't like the feeling of being lost, either."

I look at the table to hide the blood rushing to my cheeks. "I feel like an idiot, for getting so worked up over finding a taxi. But when it is your city and you are looking after a friend, you feel responsible."

I see her blink at me, her head cocking to one side, just an inch or so. Was I being presumptuous, calling her a "friend"?

She shifts in her chair to face me fully. "I'm sorry, too. I know I can't have been the easiest of people to be stuck with today." She looks at the wall and grins, shaking her head as if she cannot believe what she is remembering. "But the whole party boat thing *was* kind of funny ..."

"You will have your own unique memories of Paris, just like your mom and dad did."

I hear her take a sharp breath, her smile suddenly shakier. "I cannot imagine what it is like to grieve a parent," I tell her honestly. "For what it is worth, I admire your courage. This trip must require a lot of strength."

She looks down at the table. "It's harder because it's Christmas. *No one* loved Christmastime more than Dad. He used to get so excited that Mom had to secretly switch his coffee for decaf, just so that he had a chance of going to sleep at night. She always used to tease him, 'It's the kids who are supposed to be kept awake by their excitement ...'"

She looks past me for a moment, her eyes sparkling. A smile creeps across her face. "Wow ... I haven't thought about that in a while. Not once in the two years since he passed, but just now ... that memory, like, climbed into my head, by itself."

"It has always been there," I tell her. "It was behind a door in your mind. Because you know what is behind the door, you don't always have to look. But when you open it, it is like remembering all over again. The last time I was with my grandpapa, we were looking through old photo albums. Mama would point to this photo or that photo, and she would ask him: Did he remember this, remember that? One of the photos was of me and him at a rugby match. France versus England. So many people at the stadium, you know? I was about five years old, so my memory of that day was not clear. I ask Mama, 'What happened? Who won?,' but she could not tell me. Then, Grandpapa, he shouts so loud, I almost fall off the sofa! He tells me all about the match, every detail. How France almost won in the last few minutes, but then Jonny Wilkinson made a drop goal and England won."

It is rare that I smile while I describe France losing to England, but that's what I'm doing — smiling — while at the same time hot tears form in my eyes. All at once, I feel happy *and* sad. Memory is very strange.

"Was he right?" Serena asks. "I mean, was he remembering what actually happened?"

I shrug. "I do not know for sure. But I looked up the match, and the score was as he said. Even if he was wrong, though, I ... I would not really care. For a few moments, it felt like I had my *real* grandpapa back."

She stares at me for a long moment. Her eyes have been shimmering with tears since she started telling me how excited her father would get at Christmas. We both have one hand on the table, and I see her fingers twitch — is she thinking about reaching across and taking my hand? Before she can move, Didier is back.

"I have spoken with the chef," he tells us, setting our Cokes down on the table, "and he says, because it is Christmas, he is happy to make something for you early."

Serena looks very happy to hear this. "Oh, thank you so much," she says. "Can I please have the *blanquette de veau*?"

Veal stew must be what her parents had when they were here.

I tell Didier that I'll have the same, and he is gone as quickly as he reappeared, his *bouffant* only just about managing to keep up.

Once we're alone again, Serena looks back at her hand, sees its awkward position on the table and retracts it. "Your grandfather sounds like a great guy."

"He was."

"Hey, he's still here." She leans forward to look me in the eye, to make her point. Keeps her hands on her side of the table. "He's not dead."

I stop myself from saying he might as well be — since, most of the time, it feels like he is — and instead just let the silence play out.

When Serena's phone pings, we are both startled. "Sorry," she says, rummaging in her bag. She takes out her phone and looks at the screen as if she does not understand what she is seeing.

"Is something wrong?" I ask her.

"Uh … no … It's just a friend. From school. A friend from school."

Ah. I understand. For some reason, I can't stop myself from addressing the tabletop. "The boy from the bridge."

"Ethan. He says his friend Jesse can't make it anymore, so …"

She stares back at her phone, as if wanting to confirm that she has actually read Ethan's message correctly.

I ask, "What can't Jesse make?"

"Oh … Ethan, he" — she puts her phone back in her bag — "he has tickets. For the Eiffel Tower tonight. He just offered one to me.

He also invited me to dinner at some place called Le cygne rouge, but said that I need to get there in an hour, because that's when he's leaving."

I know the bistro. The Red Swan. It is down by Barbès-Rochechouart and is ... well, it is terrible. "That sounds nice," I say. "If you want, we can cancel the food here. Or I can eat it all ... I am suddenly very hungry."

Maybe I should dial it down a little, so that it doesn't look like I *want* her to go away. It's not lost on me that I actually got through talking about my grandpapa without falling to pieces, which is what I feared would happen if I tried, and that she accepted my simple explanations without probing, without asking more questions. We haven't had the easiest of times getting around Paris today, but — mostly — talking to Serena *has* been easy, and I'll admit to myself that I really like this about her and want it to continue for the rest of this night ...

But I know how much she wants to go to the tower. I do not want her to feel guilty about leaving.

"No," she says brightly. "That's okay. We've already ordered, and I *wanted* to eat here. This restaurant is just as important a stop on the Romance Tour as making it to the Eiffel Tower. If I rush it just so I can meet Ethan, I won't appreciate it ..." She looks down at the table, and I can tell that she is not at all certain about her decision. Then she looks up at me. "Besides, you've gone out of your way to show me around today, so the least I could do is buy you a nice dinner."

I smile and try not to look *too* happy. Then I concentrate on my Coke, picking up my glass and swirling it around.

"Sorry," she says, putting the phone back in her bag. "It was *so* rude of me to check my phone during dinner."

I give her my best smile. "Dinner has not arrived …"

"And it's probably not even 'dinner,' is it?" She makes a shocked face. "Before seven o'clock! My God!"

I do my best to laugh with her, but it's kind of awkward, and the back of my neck starts to itch a little — which always happens when I'm tense and nervous.

When I hear the whine of a door swinging open, I look in the direction of the kitchen, grateful for the distraction of Didier coming back with appetizers. But it is not the young man with the perfect *bouffant* heading over to our table.

It is Martine.

And suddenly it all makes sense to me. *That* is why the name of this place sounded familiar. Right before we broke up, Martine had an interview for a waitressing job. I feel wretched for not knowing the outcome of the interview — and I also start regretting asking for a corner table. I'm totally trapped.

✳

It is a familiar feeling, being trapped by Martine. When the spontaneous, passionate woman who so excited me when we were first together spontaneously, passionately decided to break into my dorm room and sit on my bed, waiting for me to get back from another dressing down from Monsieur Deschamps … I'd known she had pulled me over to a place I did not want to be.

"I have some things I wish to talk about." She stood up off the bed, and I became painfully aware that underneath it, right by her foot, was a shirt that she had made for me in her clothing design class.

And then she was walking toward me. "I have been thinking a lot about us, and I believe I have figured something out."

"Please don't do this," I told her. "These conversations, they never end well. We both end up depressed. You're making it harder on yourself. And you can't just *break into* dorms like this, Martine — what if one of my dormmates saw you? You could get in trouble!"

I could see in her eyes that this didn't really get through to her. The feeling of being suffocated — which I had felt fairly often when I was around her — was creeping back.

"Please just answer one question," she said. "Answer one question, and I will leave."

I doubted there could be a single us-related question that she hadn't yet asked me, but I nodded and said okay.

"What is your problem?"

"My problem?" I asked, trying not to laugh too hard. For all the stress and drama she created, I did not want Martine to think I was mocking her. She did not deserve that. "Well, I have someone sneaking into my dorm room when I'm not here. And I'm worried about you, because this is not normal behavior."

She said nothing — and when someone so talkative falls silent, it can be unnerving. Finally, she shook her head: "I didn't mean that. I meant, what is your *real* problem? The deep problem. Why are you turned off by someone wanting to be close to you?"

I couldn't give her an answer, because I had not expected the question.

"I have some work to do," was all I said. "And I know you must have work to do, as well ..."

I gestured toward the door, but she didn't move. She just sighed and put her hands on her head, the raven on her forearm suspended in flight, glaring at me.

"You are always running away," she told the ceiling. "I used to think you wanted to see if people would follow you, but now I'm not so sure. I think you might actually *like* running!"

For some reason, this prompted me to look at the floor, which I must have done for a long time, because pretty soon, Martine was shouting, over and over again: "Look at me ... Will you please ... just *look* at me, Jean-Luc? Stop running, and look ... see the person who is running with you!"

*

Now, in the bistro, I feel like I want to literally run away. But I don't. I just stare at Martine staring at me, standing as still as some of the statues in the Louvre. Then a flash of movement at the corner of my vision drags my attention to Serena, who's shifting in her chair to see who I'm staring at. She sees Martine, then looks back at me, her eyes widening, like, *Oh, God — it's the crazy ex-girlfriend from the photo!*

Martine turns to the bar and chats with the short, plump woman standing behind it.

"How rough was your breakup?" Serena mumbles to me.

I answer through the corner of my mouth: "*Très* rough ... Listen, I might have to ..."

"She's coming, she's coming!"

I wish I could say that Martine seems to walk over to us in slow motion, but real life is never so kind as to give you time and space to think. There are maybe ten yards between us and her, and she closes that distance in a few seconds flat.

"Martine ..." I can barely hear my own voice over the sound in my head, like the rushing noise you get on an airplane. I am somehow able to smile, though all I can think is, how the hell can I explain why I've brought a girl to her place of work? I'm not even sure I can tell her the truth, because, as I lay it all out in my head — random American girl turns up at my dorm, and we go on an odyssey through Paris, at *Christmas* — it seems kind of ... romantic, and I don't want Martine to get the wrong idea.

She's had enough hurt this winter.

She stops by our table. I don't like the way she's smiling, like she's happy I'm here. I also don't like that she's standing the same way Didier was when he took our order just now, barely moving with her hands behind her back. "Jean-Luc ... How nice to see you. Merry Christmas."

She's speaking English, which means that one of her colleagues must have mentioned that there's an American here. The rushing noise in my head is now almost deafening.

Martine turns to Serena, her smile so unnervingly placid that I can tell she's putting effort into it — and any smile that takes this much effort is *not* to be trusted. "I know Didier has already taken your order, but anything else you want, just ask me."

Serena hesitates for a moment, probably a little uncomfortable at meeting my crazy ex-girlfriend in a deserted restaurant in a foreign country. I feel bad that she's in the middle of this, and the way Martine is just *smiling* makes my ribs give my heart the kind of death-hug that reminds me of the hugs *she* would give me back when we first got together.

I have to get out of here — right now. If we stay, Martine will say or do something that will start another argument. I never got around to answering her question — *Why are you turned off by someone wanting to be close to you?* — and after everything she said about my always running away, my actually running now would only prove her point.

But what else can I possibly do?

"Actually," I start to say, "we were just about to tell Didier that we could not stay after all."

"We were?" That is Serena, sounding as confused as if I said this in French. I don't look at her, because I don't think I could bear to see her disappointment. It's the only thing that gives me the nerve to hold Martine's cold blue eyes.

"Would you please cancel our order?" I ask.

Martine is quiet. That always makes me nervous. Since we're talking in English, I'm choosing my words very carefully, and the deliberate way I'm speaking and enunciating, so that Martine will definitely understand, makes everything I say seem a bit colder, a bit more cutting, than I intend.

"What are you talking about?" That's Serena again. I can see her on the edge of my vision, leaning forward. Yes, it's actually easier than I expected to keep looking at Martine — the alternative is to look at Serena and confirm that I am going to ruin yet another stop on the Romance Tour.

"Yes," I tell Martine, lifting my coat from the back of my chair. "Just as we arrived, my mama texted me to say she might need some help with Grandpapa. She has been with him all day, so it is unfair of me to be out having a fancy dinner while she is stuck at home."

"But your aunt Fleur visits him every Friday" is all Martine says. I forgot how well she knows me.

"Fleur is … sick." My coat is on, and it joins my rib cage in its death-hug. I feel like I am going to either pass out or throw up. "Please extend our apologies to the chef."

I flick my eyes to Serena in a way that I hope tells her that I'll see her outside. She just looks back at me, confused and very angry.

I don't walk past Martine. Instead, I veer left, putting three rows of tables between us before I head toward the door, because what if she's holding something sharp behind her back?

Back out on Abbesses, the way the winter air slices at my cheeks feels almost pleasant, like it is scraping away the tension I'm feeling. At the same time, the dense fog seems to close around me. I see so little of the city that I start to feel claustrophobic even though I'm outside. I figure I'll be okay if I can just get away from this bistro, so I hurry down the steps to the sidewalk and along Abbesses without looking back — until I realize that Serena hasn't come out. She's not actually staying behind to eat by herself?

It's a long couple of minutes, but eventually Serena appears.

"What the *hell* was that?" she hisses.

"I am sorry —"

"No! No ..." She stomps down the steps to the sidewalk. Her cheeks are a little rosy, and it's not to do with the winter chill. She's furious. "None of your 'Iyam sorreee' bullshit. You don't get to accent your way out of this! You left me in there — I was so embarrassed, I actually paid for the food that we *didn't eat*. Jean-Luc, you *knew* how much I wanted to eat here, how ... shit!"

"What is it?"

"Shut up." She's turning around and walking back toward the restaurant. "I left my bag inside. My sister's scarf's in that bag."

The tension in my chest is back. I've really ruined this part of Serena's trip, but if she had seen how my breakup with Martine had played out, I am sure she would agree I could *not* have sat there and had her wait on me. It would also have been terribly unfair to Martine — even if she didn't spit on or poison our *blanquettes de veau*, it would have been terrible for her to have to "make nice" with her ex-boyfriend and the random American stranger he is suddenly spending the day with.

Serena takes so long to come back out that I start to worry about her. When she reappears, carrying her bag, she is silent.

"I'll treat you," I tell her. "I know just the place. My favorite bistro, in *real* Paris. You'll love it, and it'll be *yours* — you'll have your own memory of *your* Paris. Trust me ..."

I can feel the eagerness on my face, can hear the pitch of my voice. I really am trying to sell this to her. Maybe all of this awkwardness *is* actually leading us to something better, more worthwhile, more memorable?

Serena takes out her phone to check the time. "Well, I already turned down Ethan's offer … but I'm still going to have to eat something, I guess."

Satisfied, I lead Serena back down Abbesses toward the Metro station.

I did it. I got us away from Martine!

And yet, all the way there, I wonder why I feel so wretched.

~ CHAPTER NINE ~

SERENA

6:17 P.M.

I've hated Paris Metro stations since the very first time I used
one — which, admittedly, was just this morning, but still! —
and that hate is only increasing. At least the grime of the New York
subway has some character. Anvers station in Paris is just white
corridors that feel endless — so cramped that the echoes of footsteps and conversation, and the hiss and whine of the trains passing
through make me feel like I'm drowning in a *soup* of sound.

But then, maybe everything is getting on my nerves because I
can't figure out this French guy I've somehow ended up spending
all day with. First, he makes a big show about how he's happy
to eat *both* of our meals if I wanted to leave and meet up with
Ethan. Then, just a few minutes later, he's basically dragging me
out of Maison d'angle, because *he* forgot it was where his ex now
worked. I would have totally been within my rights to say, to hell

with him, and stay to eat by myself. But I couldn't have done that because, unlike Jean-Luc, I felt an appropriate amount of mortification at what was happening.

He leads me down a flight of stairs onto a platform, taking a seat on a plastic bench beside a vending machine. I take the seat next to him, even though I kind of wish I were sitting an ocean away — the opposite platform would do. Since the moment we walked away from the bistro, he's been talking about how "great" his favorite place is and how I will be craving it as soon as I'm back home, and the more he talks, the angrier I feel.

Because, for all that stuff about his grandfather, he still doesn't *really* know loss. He doesn't know what it's like to toss and turn all night because you're imagining what you would have said to your dad that morning, if you'd known it was going to be his last day on this earth.

Real loss is something I've been feeling for two years, what I've come to Paris to fix, if I possibly can. But today is close to being over, and Paris is slowly going to sleep — if the damned fog doesn't choke it out first — so all the hopes I had for this trip are slipping away. And why am I surprised by how this day has gone? If Mom and Lara couldn't understand why this trip was important to me, why did I expect this French stranger to get it?

If I'm honest, this tour was as much for me as it was for Mom. I've come here because I'm supposed to be putting together a scrapbook for my mother, so that she can remember Dad, but did *she* really need to travel to Europe to remember him? What good would it have done her to come back to this city without the man she loved, the man she associated with Paris?

But — and this is what makes me feel *really* silly — it makes sense that I would totally not get that. Because what would *I* know about real love? I've never had an actual boyfriend. I've never even *felt* anything romantic — not really. This whole mission is really just the "brain wave" of a girl who's trying to figure out what love is.

There were moments today where I felt like I was getting it. Jean-Luc would touch my hand, and for just a second, I felt like a girl in the first scenes of a great romantic story, her own lovely Paris tale, that she would tell people in the future. Just moments, just wisps — then Jean-Luc would say something annoying or something crazy would happen, and we'd be arguing again.

But the wisps were *there*. For just a second, I felt something.

But now I know Jean-Luc couldn't have felt that way. If he did ... he wouldn't have dragged me out of that bistro.

"My friends and me, we go there all the time." I tune in to Jean-Luc long enough to find out that he's still babbling on about his bistro, in "real" Paris. Why is he trying so hard to convince me the rest of this night won't totally suck?

I tune back out, start asking myself, what did I *really* want out of this trip? Did I really think that remaking the most romantic story I've ever heard was going to *show* me what love was? How did I think *that* was going to work?

I can't answer my own question, and if I wasn't in a public place, I feel like I could start crying. Because this is just a perfectly ridiculous kick in the shins from Life. "Oh, Serena," it's saying, in what I'm imagining is a reedy, nasally voice, "you convinced yourself that if you could figure out what love was, it would come to you? Oh, honey ... What gave you the idea that I was going to be fair to you? In fact, to punish you for even being optimistic, I'm going to end your very first trip to one of the greatest cities in the world with you sitting in a subway station, trying not to cry while a Very Serious French Boy rambles on and on about some restaurant to distract you from the fact that he doesn't care about you."

I've played this all wrong, right from the beginning. I came here hoping that, somehow, being in Paris would flip a switch in my head ... and that if I could *understand* love, maybe that would bring me one step closer to experiencing it.

But I still just ... don't *get* it. What if I *can't* get it? What if there's something wrong with me?

As much as I want to believe that *everyone* has a soul mate out in the world, that everyone is destined to be with one special person who is meant only for them, I grew up in New York. I've seen the blank stares of people lost in huge crowds, constantly surrounded by others while being totally alone at the same time. Some people just end up alone.

Because life is not kind to everybody.

I might have been a fool to think that Paris was going to bring me closer to the "one." Instead, it has brought me a snooty, moody French boy who is occasionally fun (when he tries to be), and is kind of talented (I think). Not that I was thinking that he was going to be the love of my life or anything, but I *was* kind of enjoying hanging out with him, at least — even if he has serious unresolved issues with Americans.

But Jean-Luc can*not* be the "one," because no "one" would ever corner me into leaving the bistro, when he knew that it was one of the major stops on the Romance Tour.

And this is who Paris has delivered — some French photographer who probably doesn't like me all that much.

"… and the *sole meunière* is incredible. You like fish, right?"

I glance at Jean-Luc sideways. His hands are gesticulating, talking up the chef as if the man's an artist, going on about his "specialty" like the dish is something on display in the Louvre.

"Are you *still* talking?" I ask him, my voice echoing through the platform. One or two commuters briefly look in our direction, then turn away.

Jean-Luc's smile doesn't waver. "What is the problem?"

"The problem? Maison d'angle was my one shot at getting the Romance Tour back on track, and you made me leave."

His smile is faltering. "I did not want you to be uncomfortable."

"*I* was fine!" A few heads turn in our direction, then away again — although, this time, I can tell at least some people are now actively eavesdropping. "It was *you* who was freaking out."

He turns his whole body to me, and for a split second, I think he's going to take my hands. But he doesn't. He just gives me a wide-eyed look that begs for understanding.

"If you knew her, you would know why I was so …" He trails off, and I wonder if he can't find the English. Either that, or he's stalling, until he can pull an excuse out of his butt. "Martine is … intense, she is emotional … She likes the drama of a breakup. If we had stayed there, your whole trip would have been ruined."

Like it hasn't been already!

"Martine would have made a scene," he goes on. "And it may

not have been me she was unhappy with. She might have made a scene with *you*."

"No one is that dramatic," I mumble, as our audience seems to tune out again, now that there's less yelling.

"You don't know her," he says. "She is not happy unless there is conflict. She needs to be worried about something, all the time. When I suggested that perhaps it would be a good idea for us to spend less time together, so that we could focus on our studies, on our art, she couldn't accept it — she assumed I was preparing to break up with her. So, do you know what she did? She said we should *move in* together. We are not even twenty years old yet! Surely you can see — it was better for us not to be around Mart —"

"That's not how Martine said it happened." The words are out before I can stop them. But I'm tired of Jean-Luc trying to justify acting like kind of a jerk. "She said she bent over backward trying to get close to you, and all you did was run away — just like you ran out of that restaurant. And, actually, she told me she's over it. She's not mad at you anymore. You'd have found that out … you know, if you hadn't run away."

He leans forward, elbows on his knees as he stares across at the opposite platform. "So, that is what took you so long to get your bag."

"She was worried about you," I tell him. "She said, when you ended it, you weren't really making sense. She thinks this whole thing with your grandfather has you all —"

"*This is none of your goddamned business!*" He's leaning away from me, glaring. And that's the loudest I've heard him yell all day.

I'd be taken aback, if I wasn't so pissed at *him*.

He's shaking his head at me. "What happened between me and Martine is between us. You should not have spoken with her about —"

"Oh, you know what? Screw you, Jean-Luc." I stand up from the seat. "*You* involved me in this by making me a part of that embarrassing scene. Also, you ruined a major part of my trip — so, honestly, I don't give a damn about your feelings right now, you *selfish* jackass."

Now it's him standing up from his seat. "I'm not keeping you hostage. You can leave anytime you like. And you've obviously *wanted* to leave ever since you ran into your American friend, so why not go to him, huh? Go to him and talk about your Kardashians or whatever you think is so important."

I don't respond. I just push past him, heading for the exit — or, *sortie*.

Jean-Luc's voice follows me. "Okay, then, go. Go to Ethan. I hope you have a wonderful time talking about … about … about what guns you will buy when you go back to college!"

I can't believe I wasted a whole day on this guy. I can't believe I was actually starting to enjoy having him around, even though he was always one snooty comment away from driving me totally nuts.

Once I'm out of Anvers station and onto a road called Boulevard de Rochechouart, I have to take a second not to freak out. The fog seems to have gotten thicker, and when other pedestrians walk by me, I feel like I'm being stalked by dozens of Grim Reapers. I turn in a circle and figure out that

I'm on an island, on a strip separating two busy roads that seem to have been designed to test the drivers, to see who's *really* concentrating. They just branch off in all directions, and I'm in such a bad mood after walking away from Jean-Luc that I kind of want to scream at *all* of Paris: Do you not see why New York thought a *grid* system was a sensible idea?

Calm down, Fuentes. I repeat this a couple times in my head, like a little mantra. I have Google Maps, so I know I'm not truly lost. I just ... have to figure out where I'm going to go first. I'm still hungry, so I take out my phone and check what's close and what has at least a three-star rating. The words "Le cygne rouge" seem to float up from my phone's screen. It's the bistro where Ethan said he was eating tonight, and it's close by.

I text him.

Hey! Are you still there?

Before I can put my phone back in my pocket, I see the three-dots-of-typing, so I keep it out as I wait for his reply. It takes a while, and my fingers start to go numb from the cold.

Yeah — where are you? x

I'm a little annoyed at almost losing my fingers to frostbite for four words. I wonder how okay it will be to ask the question I'm ramping up to asking him. But then I figure that a) seeing the Eiffel Tower might just save the Romance Tour and make all of this worthwhile, and b) Ethan will know why I'm asking, won't get the wrong idea ... and c) the worst he can do is say no, if he's offended at my asking.

> Stranded on an island — literally! But I'm not far from you.
> Is that ticket still available?

I think about adding a hopeful face emoji, but it feels like it would be silly, like I know that I'm possibly overstepping by asking. I could add an "x" at the end, but that seems all wrong, too, after the *kisstastrophe*. So I just send the message, faceless and kissless.

The reply is almost instant.

> It is, indeed! :) x

My shoulders sag with relief. Finally, a bit of luck! I follow my phone's directions, walking straight ahead, along the strip that divides the lanes of Boulevard de Rochechouart. The trees form a kind of canopy over my head, like cracks in the fog, and I think that maybe I should get myself to one of the sidewalks, which are better lit and where I will at least feel less lost. But the traffic is terrible on both lanes, and I can't see any crosswalks, so I forget that and keep walking, into the fog.

Even though so many things have gone wrong today, how this trip ends is in *my hands*. Coming to Paris might yet prove to be worth it, because I can still complete the Romance Tour.

And that is exactly what I am going to do.

*

After another five minutes of walking, the noises of Boulevard de Rochechouart become almost unbearable. Even though it's loud, and the sharp air is thick with exhaust fumes that are probably like steroids to this damned fog, I find it oddly comforting. This little corner of Paris feels a bit more like New York, and as I follow the directions on my phone to Le cygne rouge, the restaurant looks bright and welcoming, like a lighthouse offering refuge to stranded tourists. I wonder, could this be because I'm meeting up with Ethan?

Is that why I'm in a better mood?

I find him sitting at a table outside, beneath one of those heater lamps, which bathes him in a red glow that looks either gaudy or romantic, I can't really decide. He's looking, like, actually sophisticated with a carafe of red wine in front of him and an empty plate. I've missed dinner. When he sees me, he does a double take, then breaks out in the biggest smile — which, I have to say, is a very nice contrast from some of the expressions I saw on my *other* companion today.

"Serena!"

I point to the empty chair at his table. "This seat taken?"

"It is now," he says, his smile widening, getting a waiter's attention and saying something in French. When he points at me, I figure he's asking for an extra menu and wineglass.

"Oh, no," I tell him. "I don't have to eat." Why am I lying?

"We have time," Ethan says, as the waiter goes back inside. When he pushes open the door, a blast of smooth jazz escapes into the street.

The moment I collapse into the empty chair, I feel like I could pass out, and I'm suddenly *very* aware that I'm running on about three hours' sleep, which I guess I got while in a different time zone. But I can't stop now — not when I still have the last remaining scrap of the Romance Tour to get through. Not when Ethan is gazing at me the way that he is.

"I'm so glad you could make it."

I can feel the smile beaming from my face. I'm going to get to have a great dinner, with a nice guy, right before we head to the Eiffel Tower — for which fate has miraculously brought me tickets. Finally, something in this day is going right.

CHAPTER TEN

JEAN-LUC

18H54

A train — the third since Serena stormed off — pulls into the station, and a pair of drunk guys in suits stagger onto the platform, looking like they've had quite a night. One of them has a bottle of beer in one hand and is holding a mistletoe over his head with the other, looking for someone to kiss, even though there's nobody in range. His friend doubles over with his hands on his knees, like he's about to throw up. The first guy sees this and offers him the bottle, like it is some kind of medicine. It's the kind of tableau that I would normally try to photograph, but my hands don't even twitch, much less reach for my camera.

I have not moved from this seat since Serena left, but I don't know if it's because I simply don't want to, or because I am incapable. My nine-hour friendship with her has apparently been destroyed, but I am pretty certain we're going to have to see each other again at some point — she left her things at my dorm, after all. She never actually took the spare key, so if she comes back, and I'm not there, she'll have to try to explain who she is and hope whoever's at the front desk will believe her story. Or she will have to hope that someone can track me down. Either way, it'll be awkward for her. And afterward, assuming we are reunited, I just know that she will find a way to blame me for *that*, too. Because Serena seems able to get mad at me very, *very* quickly. To be fair to her, I do know it was out of line for me to expect her to leave that bistro (I may have overdone it, talking up my "better" place). I knew, as it was happening, that she had a reason to be angry with me.

But don't I have a reason to be angry at *her*? I have *wasted* the entire day, at the expense of my project! Monsieur Deschamps is going to fail me.

And I also think she knew *exactly* what she was doing when she called me "selfish." I am *not* my father.

I watch the guy with the mistletoe guide his drunker friend along to the exit, wondering how this day — which didn't promise all that much to begin with — somehow managed to go even worse than I expected.

I know it's not really Serena's fault. She did more than enough to accommodate me — even changing her plans so that I could show her the Dugarry exhibit. She cannot have *wanted* to take such time out from her Romance Tour, but she did it. Because she is a decent person. This day was going well enough until …

Martine. Martine, charging back into my life at the worst possible time, creating upheaval as she always does.

She told me she's over it. That's what Serena said. Could I have misread Martine in the bistro? What if I wasn't seeing the calm before a storm but just … calm? *Now,* suddenly, I find the energy to spring out of my chair and march toward the exit, walking so quickly that I catch up with the drunk guys in suits, who shout insults at me when I bump into them.

I cannot believe I'm heading back to Maison d'angle. Martine has already ruined one project of mine and may have helped "finish off" another. But maybe we do need to talk.

If she *has* moved on from the feelings that our breakup left behind, I would like her to tell me how she did it.

✳

Maison d'angle is very busy by the time I return. Even Didier's hair has lost some of its structure. The chatter of the patrons is so loud, I can almost feel it around my ears, but when Martine sees me lingering by the welcome desk, all that noise seems to be sucked away as she just … stares at me. Have I made a terrible mistake? I gesture to her. *Can we talk?*

She's holding two dishes, standing over a table for two. She puts the food down with a smile, shares a few words with the customers and then walks over to me. I have a little freak-out — what if she thinks I've returned because I want to get back together? That I've dumped the American girl and am now making some big, romantic gesture? Am I going to upset her all over again?

But there's no hope in her eyes. Only confusion. And maybe … embarrassment?

"Jean-Luc, what are you doing back here?"

"I need to talk to you," I tell her. "Can you take a break?"

She raises her eyebrows and jerks her head in the direction of the very crowded bistro.

"I know this is inconvenient," I tell her, "and I am sorry. But this is very important. It would mean a lot to me. To you, too, I think."

She pauses. "Okay … Go around back. I'll see you in the alley, but I can talk for a few minutes only."

"Thank you."

I walk back onto the street, then around to the alley behind Maison d'angle. Martine keeps me waiting just long enough that I start to wonder if she's going to leave me out here to get hypothermia, as some kind of revenge, but the back door opens and she comes out, shrugging on her peacoat.

"What do you want?" she asks, her pale face like a ghost in the alley.

For a second, I can think of nothing else except how strange it feels to be alone with Martine, face to face and a few feet away from each other, making very intense eye contact in the dark.

"Are you really not angry anymore?"

We have one of those long, drawn-out silences that I used to dread. I fight the urge to look away from her, seeing that her face fills not with anger or hysteria but with pity. Sympathy. "I've moved on. You should try it."

I stay quiet for so long that she sighs, annoyed.

"You make me wonder if you don't *want* me to move on or something." Does she think I might *like* the idea of her being upset? I know our fights sometimes got personal, hurtful, but she should still know me well enough to know that I do not *enjoy* seeing her miserable.

Apparently, neither of us could see how wrong we were for each other.

"You hurt me," she says. "You took everything I tried to give you, dropped it and ran away. The more I tried to close the distance between us, the faster you ran."

I look at the cobbles. "I know ... I really am sorry. About everything that happened."

"And what are you even doing here with *me* right now? You have a nice girl in your life, and you're here talking to the ex that you did not want to be with. Why?"

"I ... I don't know."

She reaches out and lightly grabs my elbow — a prompt that I should look at her. Her face is soft, understanding. Her voice is, too: "Because you want to be forgiven. I know you, Jean-Luc — I'll bet that, no matter how good a time you have had with this American girl, you have still picked fights with her. Right? It's because you need people to prove to you that they *do* want you around."

She is looking right into my eyes, unblinking. A look of this intensity sometimes makes me edgy, but now ... Now, she looks concerned, almost tender. "You do all of this to get what you want, and the minute anyone *starts* making an effort to show you they do want you, you run. I was tired of having to chase you all the time."

I don't know what to say to that, even though there's a lot I *could* say. I wish I could have made clearer to her that all those times I picked fights were not just about me testing how much she wanted to be with me. I think a part of me was excited by the thought that she might one day tell me to go to hell, so I would have a motivation to improve myself ...

A motivation I've felt sometimes today. And why would that be?

"I'm sorry, Martine ... I'm sorry I hurt you."

She just smiles — which makes it weird when she says: "You did hurt me. But I'm going to be okay. In fact" — the hand on my elbow slides up to my shoulder, friendly, appreciative ... platonic — "you might have done me a huge favor. Because I got sick of crying after about a week, and then I applied for a bunch of internships — you know, to keep myself occupied — and I got one."

"That's great." I really mean it.

"It's only a small designer in Le Marais. But I am learning so much, and it's a great experience. Plus, I'm, uh, going on a date tomorrow."

I try not to look surprised, but I can see from the way she rolls her eyes that I have failed. She laughs.

"His name is Laurent, and he's a medical student."

Now I don't even bother trying not to look surprised. "A medical student? That ..."

"Does not sound like my type?" she asks, taking a step back from me. This whole conversation is much more formal than I'm used to with Martine, but I have to admit — I kind of like not being tense all the time. "I think that is where you and I were always wrong, you know? I used to look at love like kind of a jigsaw puzzle, that you needed two pieces that were similar enough to fit together. It was only when I found that in you that I realized, we were *too* alike. Put us together, we just make the same shape, only bigger. But when you put two very different pieces together, they form something *new*."

This is the first conversation we've had in a while that's not going to end with one of us storming off. My heart hasn't felt this light since Martine and I first got together, back when …

"I *did* love you, you know?" I tell her. "I … don't want you to think I never did."

Her smile doesn't waver, but her eyes do glisten a little, and she pulls her hand back. "Thank you …" Then, she gathers herself and points at the camera I kind of forgot was still on me. "Is that your project for Monsieur Deschamps? Can I see?"

I take the camera off my neck and hand it to her, almost laughing when I realize this will be the first time she's ever held it. For various reasons, I didn't really trust her not to throw it when we were together.

Martine liked to make it clear what she thought of bad art.

She flicks through the photos I've taken today, and I brace myself for her to offer faint praise.

"They're wonderful …" she breathes.

I was not expecting this response. "What did you say?"

"I think they're lovely … especially the ones of Serena."

"Oh, those were just for fun," I say, as she hands the camera back to me. "They're not for the project."

She smirks. "But I'd say more than half the photos are of her. It's like she *is* the project … a documentary of you falling for Serena."

"I haven't fallen for her!" My voice is loud, the walls of the alley throwing my words back at me as if rubbing my face in my own lies. "She's completely wrong for me ..."

Martine just smiles as she hands me my camera. Then she leans forward and kisses me on the cheek. "Different pieces, Jean-Luc."

She turns around and walks back into the bistro, leaving me alone in the dark alley, holding my camera, which feels heavy with ... Serena.

Serena, the reason I left the dorm room at all this morning. The reason I found the will to start my project over properly, rather than try to salvage what I could from the crap I'd so far put together. Serena, who sees things in my work that even I don't notice.

A smile is breaking out on my face — I can't remember a time I was ever happy to lose an argument with Martine, until now.

Serena is *the project.*

And then I'm running out of the alley, toward the Metro. I have to get back to my dorm — right now!

~ CHAPTER ELEVEN ~

SERENA

7:35 P.M.

"It was funny until my mom called the cops!"

I'm almost choking on my veal, because Ethan is cracking me up with a story about being taken to the circus as a kid and having such a great time that he tried to sneak onto the back of one of the trucks so that he'd get taken along to the next stop. Who *is* this funny, self-deprecating guy who can make me smile even when I'm feeling kind of sad?

Ethan's laughter dies down, and for a second he just gazes at me. It makes me blush a little, and I'm about to look away, when I see his right hand stretching across the table. The tips of his fingers brush the backs of mine, before his palm — not as sweaty or clammy as I remember it being back home — settles on top of my hand.

Or it would, if I don't jerk my hand away — but I do. I try not to let my own confusion show on my face and am about to tell him, sorry, I'm just a little ticklish, but before I can, the waiter is back at our table and asking (in English, for my benefit) if we want any dessert.

"Chocolate mousse, *s'il vous plaît*" is what we *both* say, at the same time.

"Get out of my head," Ethan teases, as the waiter clears our dinner plates and heads back inside.

I return Ethan's smile, and we fall quiet once more. It's not really an intimate moment, because of the chaos of engine noises and random car horns, even a police siren, outside, but I'm surprised to realize that I'm worried I may have hurt his feelings with the whole hand-retraction thing.

Now I'm the one who reaches across the table, and when I place my hand on his, Ethan turns his over so that we're palm to palm. It might not be the sweaty, clammy palm that I remember from back at Columbia, but my whole arm instantly feels like it's made of wood, and the pressure of his hand is oddly tight.

It's just because this is new, I tell myself. *You could get used to it.*

"So, listen ..." Ethan gently squeezes my hand — I couldn't take it back now even if I wanted to. "I'm glad we managed to meet up again, because there're some things I've wanted to say to you since that party back home. In fact, I have to admit — I don't think I've ever really stopped thinking about what an idiot I was that night."

"Forget it," I tell him. But before I can say any more, he's holding up his free hand — not quite a shushing gesture, but definitely one that says, he's got more to say.

"I messed up, I was wrong. Just because *I* couldn't really see how putting yourself through all these emotions was going to help you get over what happened with your dad, that did not give me the right to judge. It's none of my business. And while I don't have much experience of grief myself, I took Psych 101 last semester, and I've read about how it can sometimes make people do ... you know, wacky things in order to heal themselves."

I don't get to respond to this ("*wacky* ...?"), because Ethan's free hand comes down, so that mine is now sandwiched between both of his palms. "Can we maybe forget all that?" he says. "Start all of this over?"

I squeeze his hand back, even though my arm is starting to cramp a little. Striking that whole hallway conversation from my memory sounds like a *very* good idea.

When I nod at him, Ethan breaks into the biggest smile I've seen since ... well, since I randomly turned up here less than an hour ago. It's nice to look at a guy who *wants* you here with him, who *wants* to talk with you.

"Awesome," he says. "Because I really do think that, tonight, I'm going to make a much better case for why we should get together."

✳

8:04 P.M.

It's not exactly elegant, ladylike behavior — and it's not like I'm super keen to eat every single last bite of my chocolate mousse

(I'm actually kind of full) — but focusing on my spoon is a way to hide my face from Ethan as he explains just how much we can save if we split all our subscriptions and memberships: Spotify, Amazon Prime, Netflix ...

Is it a bad thing that I most definitely do *not* want him to see what I put on my Netflix list?

"You mentioned you liked that hiking trip your mom took you on a couple years ago. I love hiking, too! We'd never be at a loss for something to do on weekends."

I kind of wish I didn't have my hair tied back — I could do with a veil of privacy right now, while I figure out how to respond.

"You know I don't believe in coincidences," he goes on. *Now* I look back up at him. "We're both cultured people, here for quite specific reasons, purposes — even in a world of seven-and-a-half-billion people, the probability of us running into each other was higher than you might think. It's *not* a silly twist of fate."

He's leaning forward in his chair, his forearms on the table. Excited. There is wonder in his expression — it kind of weirds me out, because it's so unlike him. And the fact that he sounds like he does when I've seen him arguing with people unsettles me. I feel like I'm ... well, maybe not on trial, but definitely in some kind of deposition.

"We weren't born for each other or anything like that," he goes on. "People change over time, they grow and develop. No one is 'born for' anybody. But there are people like the two of us who are like" — he snaps his fingers, looking away, as if he might find the right words somewhere in the stalled traffic — "like pieces of a jigsaw, you know? Pieces that are kind of the same, that fit perfectly together" — his eyes light up and he looks at me again, as if he's thought of something he thinks is great — "and make a corner. And when you're solving a jigsaw, it's best to start with the corners. It makes everything afterward much, much simpler."

But a little less exciting is what I think but don't say.

He must take my silence as agreement, because he is moving on to his next point.

"So, building out from that corner, I'd say we should give ourselves a one-year deadline. Christmas is convenient for that, right? And if we still consider ourselves broadly compatible by then, we should consider targeting the summer after sophomore year for when we might start looking for an apartment together. It would make the last two years of college a lot easier, if we're saving so much money on rent and stuff." His eyes continually flit from me to the street — well, beyond the street, to a movie screen that only he can see, playing our epically scheduled love story. "I'd say let's do it *this* coming summer, but that might not give us enough time to find a good place that we can both afford. Unless you'd be cool with moving out to somewhere like West Orange."

He says that like he's forgotten it's in New Jersey. But I guess it does make some kind of sense. It's hard to disagree with him, after listening to his near-ten-minute argument of the case. But I'm not really focusing on what Ethan has been saying about joint memberships or West Orange.

I'm thinking about that business about the jigsaw pieces, about the corners — I realize how he's looking at me, making eye contact in a way that he has never really done before. He's being physically forward in a way that's unlike him, too. There'd be no *kisstastrophe* today, I can tell. All this talk of planning for a future ... *this* is what excites Ethan. I was wrong before, when I thought that he had no poetry or romance in his soul — he just has a very particular kind of poetry and wants a very particular kind of romance.

But there's a way that he's looking at me right now. His eyes are not asking me what I want — he's asking me, do I agree? Do I agree about how much we have in common, all the things that make me a "good fit" for his imagined future?

Suddenly, it feels like the fog is not only strangling Paris but poor American girls *in* Paris, too.

Ethan's still talking: "I figure, by the time I've graduated, we could look to move back into the city — or at least closer to it, so my commute isn't so bad. Whatever job I have after law school is going to be tough enough without spending an hour on a train every morning. But if we do that, we probably shouldn't go anywhere too fancy, because we'll probably be saving for a bigger place by then ..."

I know where he's going with this ... Oh, God.

"Unless, you know, you haven't really thought about at what age you'd like to start a family?"

Of course I haven't. I'm eighteen, and there are *literally* hundreds, maybe thousands, of things for me to think about before I get to that. How did our surprisingly fun dinner turn into some weird future where I'm married to a lawyer and we're thinking about kids?

The only thing I can think to do is laugh and hope I don't

somehow choke on the fog. "Let's maybe not get ahead of ourselves, huh?"

I worry this might read to him as dismissive or even mocking, but he doesn't seem bothered at all. He just raises his hand to call for the check, and I realize I'm going to have to plead a stronger case when debating with a law student.

＊

8:22 P.M.

The dinner might be over, but as we head along Boulevard de Magenta, toward Gare du Nord station (where it'll be easier to catch a cab), Ethan is still debating whether we'll be able to afford to live in Manhattan seven years from now. He's so into his spiel that I have to reach out and grab his arm to stop him from accidentally ruining a photograph being taken by a thirty-something man who gets dangerously close to the curb as he tries to get a shot of his three friends. They're all in thick winter coats posing outside a wedding tailor's shop. A groom and his wedding party, I guess, shopping for their outfits. (I wonder if the wedding is on New Year's Day.)

The guy taking the photo thanks us in French. As we resume walking, I notice that Ethan lightly extends his elbow toward me. Since I'm holding on to him already, I go with it and slip my arm into his, and I guess we're going to walk the rest of the way to the station like this.

It hits me only when we've reached the corner along the

roundabout that will take us to Gare du Nord that the tailor shop we passed was called "Jean-Luc." And now I'm wondering what he did after I stormed out of Anvers. I don't think he would have gone to his "better" bistro in "real" Paris by himself. He just wanted to get away from his ex. He wasn't even all that hungry. It was scandalously early, after all!

No, I bet he went back to his dorm and got all moody. Maybe smoked a cigarette and stared out the window, contemplating life and other deep, not-trivial stuff. That's what French guys do for fun on a Friday night, right?

Why the hell are you wondering about what Jean-Luc might be doing? He has impeded the Romance Tour at every turn — sometimes accidentally, sometimes *on purpose*. He should not be on my mind when, right now, the guy who rode to my rescue — offering up his spare ticket to the Eiffel Tower, of all things — has just bought me an amazing dinner and spent a long time talking about how great our future could be. Why am I thinking about some guy I've found it very easy to bicker with? Even during our late breakfast in the café, when we'd known each other less than three hours, we started needling each other, and every conversation since has felt like one blunt comment or French "*pfft!*" away from becoming a kind of fight. Is it because fighting is not always about a personality clash or a conflict but occasionally a yearning?

Charlotte had said that to me the night everyone got back to campus after Thanksgiving. Charlotte had been staying with her boyfriend, Anthony, and his family, and I don't know what happened between those two that weekend, but she seemed in a contemplative mood. I figured she and Anthony had had some heavy discussions.

We were sitting on the floor between our beds, playing poker for peanuts (literally!), when I dared to ask her if she and Anthony were heading for Splitsville. They'd been fighting a lot.

"Only about stupid stuff," she said. "We're not angry with each other so much as annoyed. When we yell, it's really that we're saying, 'Be better,' you know?"

"Sounds like a *lot* of trouble," I said.

Charlotte laughed. "Being alone is easy. Being with someone means you have to deal with them. And *that*" — she made her point by laying down her cards (sixes and sevens) — "is your problem, Serena. You want to be with someone, but you want it to be simple and easy. You need to ask yourself, is simple and easy really what's best for you?"

That was a month ago, and I still haven't figured out the answer to that question. Why would I want to be with someone I argued with all the time? That wasn't how it was for Mom and Dad — I don't think I ever heard either one of them raise their voices at each other. At me and Lara, for sure — especially Lara — but never each other.

"Serena?"

I don't know how long we've been stopped, but Ethan and I are now at Gare du Nord in a line for taxis, and he's is looking right at me, curious and a bit concerned. I blush, feeling a little guilty, almost as if he might sense that being with him prompted me to remember *that* discussion with Charlotte.

But Ethan doesn't seem to pick up on any of this. "I know this might not be the best time or place to ask, but … heck, why not?

Do you agree? We should get together? See how things go?"

What do I say to that? Twelve hours ago, I would have said, "Probably not, Ethan — the *kisstastrophe* and everything." But I've spent most of today feeling pretty alone. Walking in my parents' footsteps has been a constant reminder that the kind of connection they had is one that only a lucky handful of people in the world ever get to have and I sometimes worry I might never have. Have I been chasing something that doesn't exist? I was starting to believe that when the simple and easy guy appeared out of the blue and invited me to the top of the Eiffel Tower.

Ethan reads my hesitation as a bad sign. "Not that I'm trying to put you on the spot or anything," he says.

Um, he totally has put me on the spot.

The taxi line shuffles forward, and I tug Ethan's sleeve. "Can we see how the next few hours go?" I ask. "Before we commit to the next few years?"

Ethan smiles with his mouth but not his eyes. Finally, we reach the front of the line. We get into a taxi, and Ethan speaks to the driver in French, asking to be taken to "Tour Eiffel." I unhook my cross-body bag and place it between my feet as the driver turns up the radio, which is tuned in to what sounds like a soccer match.

The taxi pulls away from Gare du Nord and merges into the traffic. The amber glow of streetlights swoops over our faces in rhythmic waves, and eventually Ethan shifts to face me.

"Look, I'm happy to take things slow, if that's what you want, but — just for the record — I know we're a great match. I've known it since the first day of classes. The amount of stuff we have in common, the ways in which we're alike, it's almost funny —

because there's so much, it's ridiculous. You're awesome, in all the right ways. I don't think I'm going to need any more time to make my decision. I think I've already made it."

He turns to face forward again. I stare at his profile, as I get some weird tingly feelings in my belly. Not butterflies — or even excitement, really — but having someone say something like that to me does feel kind of nice. And we're in Paris, at Christmastime, heading to the Eiffel Tower — we're having a moment, right? It's definitely a story we can tell in the future.

I hesitate for a second but then take his hand, and …

I don't know what I was expecting. Not fireworks, but maybe a swelling or a quickening of the pulse. There's none of that. I tell myself that Mom and Dad weren't touchy-feely, lovey-dovey all day, every day, but that didn't mean they didn't love each other. In fact, it was the way they were so comfortable around each other that showed me they were always in love.

Ethan is beaming. I smile back at him, tell myself that I need to be here. Be present. I'm sharing the final stop on the Romance Tour with someone who is *here* for me … who could be the right guy for me …

So why am I thinking about someone else?

CHAPTER TWELVE

JEAN-LUC

20H12

My dorm room is a mess — lengths of string run from wall to wall, and I move quickly through the room, hanging printouts of the photos I've taken today with paper clips because I don't have any clothespins.

When I'm finished, I step back to the door frame so I can view the whole room. It kind of looks like I live with Sherlock Holmes — except that the images are not crime-scene photos of dead bodies or random pieces of evidence.

They are photos of Serena, mostly. Beginning with her in the courtyard of the Louvre, just outside the pyramid, averting her gaze as she thinks about her father, and what this city meant to him. In each one that follows, a shred or a suggestion of Paris hovers in the background — sometimes in focus, other times blurred like it is under water. Like the city is somehow decorating *her* as her heart continues its quest to get away from the pain that brought her here in the first place. The photos form the story of her day, a sequence capturing all the emotions that she felt as she set about her Romance Tour. Still, I think something is missing.

It is then my eye goes to a few rejected photos, placed carelessly on my nightstand, because I did not think they were right for the project — they did not fit the theme. But something is drawing me to them now, and I walk over …

They're the photos of the noticeboard for "Lonely Hearts and Missed Connections" that I slyly took while we were in Shakespeare and Company …

To H.,
I will never understand how I can see you
every day and still feel like I miss you.

To my dumpling,
even sardines taste different now.

To Adam,
I wish you all the happiness in the world,
but I could not make the memory of
seeing you marry someone else.
Please forgive me

S:
I feel like I chased you all over the
world. I just wish I now knew
how to get home

Is there anyone in Paris who wants to
have coffee and talk about botany?

K,
At first, I thought you had intruded on
my life. It's only now I realize my life
was on pause, waiting for you —
now, it is stopped.

I don't know if it was Paris that
healed my heart, or if it was you.

I read each message a couple times. I have to squint and hold
the image right up to my face to see some of them, and there are
at least three with handwriting so messy that I give up.

Each one is a message from one sad heart to another, all of
them very specific. But, altogether, the noticeboard feels like a
single message, just for me — telling me something I didn't know
I already knew.

It's better to reach out to someone, than to always be running
away.

~ CHAPTER THIRTEEN ~

SERENA

8:39 P.M.

The Eiffel Tower feels very familiar from all the photos I've seen, but the sight of it still takes my breath away — with its lights on, it looks like a sword of fire rising up out of the ground, even the fog hanging back warily, like it doesn't want to get burned. Near the very top, two thin beams of light turn slow circles, as if searching for someone who's hiding out in the city. All around me on Pont d'Iéna, tourists and locals slow down to crane their necks and gawk It's magnificent. Amazing. And I'm not just tingling with awe but sagging with relief — at last, something has gone perfectly today. I am going to get to complete my parents' Paris trip for Dad. A part of him will make it to the top of the tower, after all.

"Serena — slow down, wait for me!"

I stop so suddenly that the stream of tourists heading for the crossing at the foot of the bridge breaks apart like a wave. I force myself to turn around (which isn't easy, given what's on the other side of the street) and see that Ethan is just finishing up paying the taxi driver.

To my left, a crêpe stand and a small souvenir hut look almost embarrassed by the gaudy carousel that's behind them. To my right, a stone column topped by a statue of a man walking a horse (they're both naked — obviously) obscures my view of what I know from my research to be the Trocadéro, where we were just driving in the taxi. Ethan tried to run down some facts and trivia about it, but I wasn't listening. I'm sure it's great, but it wasn't what I was here for.

Am here for.

I raise a hand in a kind of "Sorry" gesture, then turn back, taking a deep breath to let the sight wash over me again, hoping it's as awesome as it was before Ethan distracted me. Before I can reabsorb the view, he appears on my right.

"Hey," he says. I mumble "Hey" back, as I shift my cross-body bag to my right side. It makes holding hands with Ethan a little awkward as we take the crossing, but I'm barely thinking about that right now. The closer we get to the tower, the more my body floods with adrenaline — no way do I feel like I got in on a red-eye this morning.

Finally, we've crossed the six lanes of traffic. I quickly get a sore neck from walking with my head leaned back so I can take it all in. I can't help noticing that, up close, all this tangled iron looks kind of … ugly. But it gets a pass, because it's the Eiffel Tower! I see a line of people waiting to be admitted, and my legs seem to move independently, running toward it …

Well, I *would* be running toward it, if not for Ethan keeping a firm grip on my hand and tugging me back.

"Let me get a picture first," he says, reaching into his coat and taking out his phone. I try to ignore the flush of disappointment I feel in my chest — a cell-phone camera is not exactly going to get the best-quality shot of me in this world-famous landmark.

But I tell myself, it's not about the quality of the photo — it's about capturing *the moment.*

Ethan walks backward, away from me, and I try to stay loose, like in the other photos I've "posed" for today.

"What are you doing?" Ethan asks. "Why are you looking up like that?"

"That's kind of what I was doing before you wanted to take the picture," I tell him. "It's the Eiffel Tower — I should look at it, right?"

"Why don't you just look *here*, at me?" he says, dropping into a crouch and turning his phone sideways. "That's how photos are supposed to be."

I look at him.

He doesn't take the photo. He points toward my hips. "Could you just …?"

I take my hands out of my pockets, let them hang by my sides.

"And smile …"

Being asked to smile suddenly makes my facial muscles get a little tight, but I do my best. As soon as his phone flashes, I relax and start to turn and walk toward the line again.

"Ah, damn …" I hear him mumbling. I turn back, seeing him still crouched, looking at his phone with a grimace. For a guy who's so convinced I'm his matching jigsaw piece, he's not shy about letting me know I am not all that photogenic.

"Let's get one more," he calls out, "but this time, maybe untie your hair?"

I laugh. "That won't make it any less of a mess."

"Then what about that scarf you bought," he says, pointing at my cross-body bag. "Put that on, you'll look all cool and Parisian."

"It's a photo of me at the *Eiffel Tower*," I say, using both hands to point to the world-famous landmark right above us and — for a split second — kind of hoping Ethan has the presence of mind to take a photo *right now*. "How much more Parisian can it get? Besides, I got the scarf as a joke for my sister — I was never going to wear it."

"Come on, it'll be fun and ironic, right?"

"Okay …" I reach into the bag and take out the scarf. It is just one photo, I guess. When I've put it on, I do my best to strike a pose — I stand with my feet wide apart, hold on to the edges of the scarf, look right at the camera and give a big smile.

Ethan misses the one-second window he has to take the photo while my smile looks natural. He just frowns at his phone — at me *on* his phone. "You sure you don't want to try it with your hair down?"

"I'm getting kind of cold here," I say.

Another flash, and this time, he stands up. He nods at his phone as he draws level with me. "Cool. Look."

He turns his phone so I can see the shot. Everything is perfectly framed, even if the fog looks thicker and grayer than it does in real life. The way I'm standing dead center in front of the arch formed by the tower's base, with fiery light falling over me, does look kind of cool — but there's something off. It's not just that Ethan appears to have taken the photo the second my smile started to freeze.

For some reason, I almost don't recognize myself.

"Now get one of me," he says, taking the spot where I was just standing and *almost* making a shooing gesture as he signals that I should step back. When I'm in position, he stands perfectly still, hands hanging by his side, big smile, all of his attention on the *camera*, not the sight — the photo serving only as proof that he visited the Eiffel Tower, rather than capturing whatever experience he might have been having. What would Jean-Luc say about this?

He is here just to be here.

After I've taken the photo, I hand the phone back to him, and Ethan suggests we take a selfie together.

"We've got time for that," I tell him, maybe a little quickly. "The tower's not going anywhere, right?"

He grins at me. "Of course!" Then he positions himself on my left, so that he can take the hand not blocked by my cross-body bag, and — at last! — we join the line.

We stand in silence for a little while. The line isn't moving at all, and I start to feel nervous and tense, because I can only think of asking Ethan how his trip has been, but I really don't want to have small talk. I'm standing in line for the Eiffel Tower, at Christmas — whatever we talk about should be meaningful, right? I reach across with my free hand to tap on Ethan's arm and get his attention. His reaction is ninja-quick, reaching out to take my second hand so that both are now braced in his.

"Hey, when we get back to New York, will you help me with my scrapbook? I think Mom will love it, and it'll be a way of honoring Dad. A way of making clear, he's still kind of with us, you know? And it really does work, too, because up until I got here, I felt like the whole family was kind of forgetting him. We weren't trying to do that, but his presence has been sort of fading, becoming a kind of" — (*wisp*) — "ghost in our memories. But today, I feel like I've been able to see my dad's face, how it was, how I remember it. I figure, if I can nail this scrapbook, then maybe we won't have to worry about losing our memories of him, you know?"

"Yeah, yeah, I get it," he says, now eyeballing a couple, not much older than us, a little way up the line but just on the edge of it. He's trying to figure out whether they're cutting. It seems to take a big effort for him to look back at me long enough to say: "Memories fade over time, though. It's natural that you guys will forget him, a little. Don't you think that, by trying so hard to hang on to them, you might be hurting yourself more?"

I have to focus to ignore the voice in my head that's trying to tell me something. *I've come this far. And he's not going to change my mind, anyway.*

"I can't imagine anything worse than forgetting my dad," I say, faking like I need to check my phone, so that I have an excuse to take back one of my hands. I make out like I'm surprised there's nothing there, then put my phone in my bag and keep the hand to myself. "I miss him every day — and I'll be honest, I've missed him more than ever since I got here. Really, this day has kind of been more sucky than fun" — I don't have time to answer his flinch with anything reassuring right now — "but the good moments have mostly been when something has made me feel close to him." And singing on the party boat ... but I'm not going to tell Ethan *that* story. "I want to hold on to all of them."

He's still eyeballing the cutters, but he squeezes my hand and holds me closer. I guess he's trying to be encouraging. "Reality isn't fair, Serena. You have your own life, your own future. Do you ever think that maybe *that's* the thing you should be trying hard to remember?"

I'm glad he's not looking at me right now — because I think the disappointment on my face would totally crush him. Ethan just *doesn't get it*. The weird thing is, he's *right* — of course dwelling on how much I miss Dad is going to make me sad, of course I *should* be trying to get on with my life. But he told me this in such a casual way, like he was recommending I take an umbrella with me because it might rain. Did it ever occur to him that I might simply be hurting?

"Hallelujah!" he cheers, as the line shuffles forward, slowly. And I'm realizing that what doesn't move slowly is life. The two years since Dad passed away feel like nothing, and what about the next two years? Will I wake up tomorrow, a college junior, wondering how I came to be living with the wrong guy ... in West Orange!?

"This light show is supposed to be phenomenal," Ethan is saying now. "They say that, from the tower, it will look like the lights are bathing the whole city, first in the French tricolor, then red and green ... I guess, because it's Christmas."

I don't know how great it's going to look, though, with all the fog. Wonder what Ethan will say when things don't go according to plan.

"Word is, they are going to do something similar at the Colosseum in Rome next year. Maybe we could check it out?"

I don't say anything. The line shuffles forward some more, but now my legs barely move. I'm remembering again that night after Thanksgiving, Charlotte and me in our dorm, Charlotte asking if I really thought "simple and easy" was what was best for me.

"Simple and easy" has gotten me to the Eiffel Tower, which was the Big Finish to the Romance Tour. Because of "simple and easy," I now have a shot at making sure a piece of Dad makes it here, as he planned to twenty-five years ago. I might now get the perspective — literally and figuratively — to understand what it meant to my parents to be in this city together.

Together …

They were here together. The two of them. All right, they didn't make it to the tower, but what are the stories they told me? Mom forgetting the reservation and them ending up at Maison d'angle; the silly scarf; Mom buying Dad caffeinated coffees even after his usual one o'clock cutoff, because he was struggling so much with jet lag. The way they laughed about it later, whenever they brought it up, because what they remembered was not so much the city as the joy of being there with each other.

I'm starting to see why Mom made no effort to get out of her conference.

Paris without Dad was going to be too hard for her.

My parents got to experience this city with *the One.*

That is *not* what I'm doing. I'm here with the nice, simple and easy guy, and I'm feeling shitty, because I'm hurting both of us right now.

We shuffle forward until we're next in line for the elevator that will take us up. The guard at the front of the line asks Ethan for our tickets, which Ethan took out of his coat pocket about fifty feet ago. He hands them over for inspection, then looks at me happily. I try to match his happiness but can feel that I'm not really succeeding — once again, everything around me feels distant, like a photocopy of itself. Like I'm not really here. Because even though he's looking right at me — which he's done a lot tonight — I still feel like he doesn't *see* me.

We don't see each other.

The guard hands back the tickets, then says something into the walkie talkie pinned to his collarbone. A few seconds later, he nods to Ethan, and the elevator doors open with a scraping groan and an echoing clatter that make me flinch. I can feel my hand squeezing Ethan's, but not from excitement or anything like that — suddenly, every part of me wants to pull back, to get away from here. But Ethan is already walking toward the elevator, and I'm being led along.

I lean back to sink my weight down to my feet. Ethan is already inside the elevator when he realizes what I'm doing.

He narrows his eyes at me, his jaw setting and his teeth clenching — he's confused about why I'm suddenly pulling away from him, and I can tell he's dreading what I am going to say.

His hand goes limp, and I slide mine out.

"I'm so sorry ..." I say as the elevator doors begin to close. I turn away from the Eiffel Tower and walk past the guard. He calls out something in French to me, but I don't look back.

*

As soon as the traffic lights turn red, I run across Quai Branly, take the stairs down to the riverbank and don't stop running until I'm underneath a bridge — Pont d'Iéna — that arches across the Seine like a stone canopy.

It's almost totally dark, the light from Quai Branly deflected by the bridge and cutting a lazy zigzag pattern on the Seine. The rippling water nudges the small flight of steps that leads off the bank, as if it's thinking about flooding the city. The fog stops on either side of the bridge, pondering whether it wants to crawl beneath the bridge with me.

I walk forward and slump down onto the top step. A group of well-dressed office types walk by me, and I wonder if they're on their way to a Christmas party. I bet none of them are going to find themselves on board a *not* tour boat, being forced to sing a Christmas song because they look like someone who sounds like someone famous.

God, that was so crazy. Absolutely humiliating when it happened, but I have the feeling that, when I get back to campus and Charlotte asks me about Paris, that story is going to be one of the first that I'll tell. How I was so keen to do a boat tour, I totally ignored all the warning signs that we were getting on the wrong boat. How much fun I had dancing with French strangers and sipping champagne with Jean-Luc …

And now I'm laughing, because that was *funny*. I think I even knew that it was at the time — between the mortification when we were thrown off and the dread of being in a part of Paris that even Jean-Luc didn't really know, there was a moment where I thought, *This is so ridiculous, so insane ...* And I actually wasn't thinking about the Romance Tour, wasn't missing Dad, wasn't feeling abandoned by Mom or Lara ... I was just being here, experiencing something and laughing about it. Making a memory. Like, *Hey, remember that time we accidentally gate-crashed some corporate Christmas party boat?*

I wince at my mental use of "we." What, do I expect to be reminiscing about this with Jean-Luc in the future?

He's definitely not smiling over any part of the day we spent together. I'd be surprised if he's thinking about anything other than how I told him he was selfish, knowing that I was using the same word he used to describe his father. I mean, I did have a right to be mad — he had forced me to leave Maison d'angle — but I'll admit that was a low blow.

My vision swims with tears. Would this day have gone better if I hadn't so easily gotten into arguments with Jean-Luc? Is it my fault that I've ended up alone — again, as always — today?

Another party boat crawls by, blaring some French pop song that's so absurdly upbeat, all I can do is laugh bitterly and take out my cell phone to check the time.

The Romance Tour: officially canceled at 9:06 p.m.

I'm about to put my phone back into my bag, when my eyes fall on the Eiffel Tower scarf. For some reason, the fact that I was able to get only one lame, tacky souvenir makes me feel the failure of this trip even more than getting nothing at all. Now, whenever I look at the scrapbook, I'm going to notice the absence of actual keepsakes along with the crap photos of a foggy Paris …

I need to stop thinking about my failures. I need to feel better. I need to call Mom.

"Serena?" Mom's voice drops into a baritone — which it always does when she's concerned about me. It's her version of Dad's narrow-eyed suspicion. "What's wrong?"

"Next time I say I've got a great idea" — I hold the phone away from my voice for a second, so she won't hear the gross sound of me wiping my nose — "I want you to say 'O Holy Night.'"

"Why?"

"Because, from now on, that's going to be our code for 'most epic of epic disasters…'"

When I lift the phone back to my ear, she's in the middle of saying something consoling: "… feel better when we're all together in London, I promise. I *promise*." She sighs, the noise crackly. "I knew Paris would be too hard for you … I should have tried to talk you out of doing this, and I'm sorry I didn't try harder, sweetie."

"It's not your fault, Mom. You know what I'm like when I get something in my head. I just didn't think anything could ever go *this* wrong." Then I go into full brain-dump mode, running through all my ambitious plans for the Romance Tour and how almost every stage was totally ruined.

"And I have *literally* just come from the Eiffel Tower. I was there less than ten minutes ago, and I was with Ethan — you know, that guy from school, I might have told you about him?"

"The *kisstastrophe* guy, yeah." There's a chance I might tell my mom too much.

"We had tickets," I go on, "and we were about to get on the elevator to go up, and I was thinking I was about to do something great for you and Dad, make sure that a part of him finally *did* make it to the Eiffel Tower ... but I couldn't do it, Mom."

"Oh, honey, you shouldn't feel bad about that. It's understandable if this trip made you just too sad."

I'm quiet for so long, Mom starts calling my name like we've been disconnected.

"I'm here," I say, my voice wet and croaky. "I'm sorry I badgered you about the Romance Tour — it didn't occur to me just how hard it could have been for you. I'm sorry."

"Sweetie, you don't have to apologize to me. You were trying to do a nice thing."

"That's just it ... I said this trip was about honoring Dad, putting together the scrapbook — but do you know something?"

I fall quiet, my jaw clenching — like my mouth refuses to say the thing I'm about to say.

"Honey? Talk to me. Now." Mom's really worried. I can hear it in her voice — whenever she's short and sharp, that's what it means. "What is it?"

"I ..." I take a deep breath, now grinding my teeth together like I'm trying to break them all. "I can't, Mom ... It's too horrible."

"I'm sure it's not."

I realize full tears started streaming down my face at some point. I didn't notice. I've been too busy feeling the hot fire crawling up out of my heart, into my throat.

I wipe my eyes again, but they instantly refill. "I came here for Dad — and you — and I was so excited to come here and see everything you guys saw, pay some kind of tribute to your marriage and hopefully put together a great keepsake so that we could all remember him, but ... I actually *forgot* him today. There was, like, an hour or so — I was on this boat, drinking and dancing, having a good time, and I did not think about Dad once. Isn't that horrible?"

Mom says nothing, and I'm picturing her giving her hotel room a stern look, as if I was there for her to scold.

I can't bear the silence, so I fill it. "Of course it's horrible. What kind of 'grieving' daughter forgets about her dad, just because she's having fun on some party boat? The kind who *says* she's making a present for her family but is really hoping that if she relives her parents' romantic story, she might somehow teach herself what love is actually about. That's who."

It's only now I realize that I've been feeling a little tight, a little tense, all day, and that perhaps this was because I felt bad that the Romance Tour had a kind of selfish motive. It feels good to admit this to Mom, but I start laughing at myself.

"Ugh, that's so lame, right? 'Poor me, I've never had a real boyfriend — maybe going halfway across the world will fix that.' Well, I went halfway across the world and randomly ran into my perfect match, and it *still* didn't feel right, so I have no clue what I'm going to do now."

Mom finally speaks and doesn't sound mad. I almost resent her for forgiving me, for loving me so much. "If it didn't feel right, then he *wasn't* your perfect match."

"Mom, you haven't met this guy. He likes most of the things I like, he's as organized as I am" — well, as organized as I *like* to be, when life and circumstances and plan-ruining French guys aren't getting in my way — "he wants the same things out of life that I do. We'd be like you and Dad — we'd never have an argument."

Now it's Mom who's laughing. "It's good that you can still make jokes, sweetie," she says. "That tells me you're going to be okay."

"What do you mean?"

"Wait, you were serious? You really think your dad and I never had fights?"

"Well, yeah ..."

Now she's laughing even harder. "Oh, Serena ... Your dad and I had arguments."

"What?"

"All the time! You girls never heard us, because we had a rule about not raising our voices at each other, but some nights after you were in bed, we would have some pretty serious fights. It's funny to me now, we would have them in whispers, but they were fights, nonetheless."

I try to speak but only strangled noises come out of my mouth. Finally, I manage: "I can't believe you hid them from us."

"Oh, seriously, you should be glad we did. Before you girls were born, your dad and I could really go at each other. It's hard for kids to see this in their parents, because you think of us as a single parenting unit, but your dad and I were really very different, and sometimes that meant we just annoyed the hell out of each other. So, yes, we did used to fight. In fact, I think ..." Mom stays silent so long, I think I've lost her. "Yeah, I think it was a fight in Paris that convinced us we needed to find a different way of having our disagreements."

I can feel my jaw gaping — I'm totally stunned by what I'm hearing right now. "What happened?"

"On our last day in Paris, we had such a huge fight and got so mad at each other, we actually needed a break. So we stormed off and didn't talk for about a day ... Because of that, we" — she can barely speak for laughing now — "we missed out on getting to the Eiffel Tower."

I have to press my phone to my cheek to make sure it doesn't slip out of my frozen hand. The way my luck has been today, I wouldn't be surprised if it bounced all the way into the river. "*That's* why you never made it?" I ask Mom. "Because you had a fight?"

"Yep ... Still think our honeymoon was the most romantic ever?"

"You missed the Eiffel Tower to *spite* each other?" This whole story sounds so unlike my parents, it's making me wonder if I'm still asleep on my flight, and this is all some weird fever dream.

"Oh, no, it wasn't spite — we just couldn't stand to be around each other after an argument. We always needed about six hours or so to really calm down. And do you know something? Twenty-five years later, I honestly can't remember what that fight was even about. We'd been needling each other all day, about lots of things — I was mad at your dad because he forgot to book tickets for the Musée d'Orsay, even though he knows how much I love Van Gogh, and your dad ... Huh ... That's what it was. Your dad made some joke about how I only ever got into Van Gogh to impress my high school boyfriend, Gerald, who was an artist." She goes quiet for a second, and I can picture her staring into space, remembering that day. I can tell from her voice that she's got a sad smile on her face, and I wish my arms were long enough to reach London.

Or that I was just *in* London, so I could hug her.

"*That's* why we missed the tower," Mom goes on. "Whenever your dad started thinking or talking about Gerald, you could guarantee that we'd soon be yelling at each other."

"He was jealous?" I ask.

"Back then, he was," Mom admits. "I think us missing the Eiffel Tower bothered him so much, he realized he was only causing problems by being jealous. He never got mad about Gerald after that — in fact, a few years later, we all went to a high school reunion, and the two of them got along great."

I take a deep breath. Try not to sound as shocked as I feel. "But why did you guys always talk about Paris so much, when you had such huge fights and never got to see all the things you wanted to?"

"Because even a few months after we got back, it was all we could talk about." I can hear in her voice that Mom is still smiling, but it's not a sad smile now. "Yeah, we missed a few things, but would we have preferred to stand in front of a few Van Gogh paintings for an hour when, all those years later, we were telling people how amazing Maison d'angle was? Or about how I had to eat a second dinner on our first night there because your dad mistakenly ordered clams and was too proud to admit to the waitress that he didn't really speak French?" I laugh with her. Dad was allergic to shellfish. "For us, it wasn't the sights — it was being together that made it special. I would probably not remember how I felt staring at a Van Gogh, no matter how great the art. But I'll never forget the joy of just being with the person I loved in some random corner restaurant, half the world away from home."

I stand up, because my butt is kind of going numb from sitting on this cold step for so long. "All this time," I say, "I thought everything was perfect, beginning with your honeymoon."

"It was perfect to us. And that's kind of all that really matters."

"So it didn't matter that you weren't always the best fit for each other?"

Mom's voice is soft, at once firm and comforting. "Honey, people are perfect fits only when they're in the movies. In real life, relationships require effort. When it's right, it's worth it."

"But how do you know when it's right?"

"You don't, not always. It's a gamble. But it pays off. Your dad might be gone, but I will never, ever feel cheated, because being married to him brought more good into my life than losing him has taken away."

I can feel more tears streaming down my cheeks as Mom talks, my head and my heart feeling so much lighter. My mother may be in London, and my sister in Madrid, but I no longer feel stranded and alone in a foreign city.

Even though it's not in the way that I planned, Paris has fixed my family this Christmas.

I tell my mom that I love her, miss her and will see her in London tomorrow. She tells me the same, then:

"Wait, before you go …"

"Yeah, Mom?"

"What you were saying earlier, about forgetting your dad for an hour?"

Crap, I forgot I was due a ticking off. "I know, I know," I tell her. "It won't happen again, I promise."

"I wasn't mad at you for that. Truth be told, I was happy to hear it."

"You were?"

I hear a strangled sob. Now it's Mom who's crying. "Sweetie, you don't know what it's been like these past two years, watching my happy, sweet little girl suddenly change. You used to smile so much — all the time — and now you don't. And I couldn't *do* anything to make you smile, and it broke my heart, every day … Because I know you were just trying not to show me how sad you were — but that never meant you couldn't be *happy*. And for a while, I've wondered if you ever *could* be happy again, because you seemed so … I don't know, like …"

"Like I'm not really here?" I give her the words I think she's searching for. The words that seem to have come up more than a few times today.

"Yes."

"You don't have to worry about that," I tell her. "Never again."

We finish our goodbyes. I end the call and stand in the darkness beneath Pont d'Iéna, letting the tears flow, feeling like the tension and grief are draining out of me, the same way the Paris fog finally seems to be lifting.

When I put my cell phone back in my cross-body bag, I see

that tacky scarf again. Jean-Luc might have been too generous when he said it was worth five euros.

I ball it up and throw it into the Seine. I'm going to leave Paris with *my own* memories, not forgeries of the ones my parents made on their honeymoon. No more walking in anyone else's footsteps — from now on, I walk in *my* footsteps, and those footsteps have to be taking me *forward*.

And even though the conversation with Mom has left me kind of drained, I find the energy in my legs to run out of the shadows of the bridge, into the light of Quai Branly, toward Pont de l'Alma Metro station.

CHAPTER FOURTEEN

JEAN-LUC

21H40

It's a shame I can't just move my whole dorm room to Monsieur Deschamps's office and present my project, rather than take everything down and put it in a folder. From the doorway, it looks kind of great — all my photos of Serena arranged in chronological order, the occasional "Lonely Hearts and Missed Connections" note pasted into a corner, like a commentary. I'm surprised at how well they fit together — like how the shot I got of her in the Louvre, among the dense crowd in front of the *Mona Lisa*, her eyes cast down so that she would not see the painting until she was close, somehow matches the anonymous, barely legible scrawl of someone writing to a "Sabine":

I don't want to look up if I know you're not there.

Or how the photo of Serena staring at the Seine, tears streaming down her cheeks as she began to open up about why she had come to Paris, feels like an illustration of a message from "Z" to "Patrice":

My heart is heavy with the goodbye I never got to say.

In the photo, the river disappears into the fog, seemingly infinite but also a dead end, like a veil Paris has thrown over itself, so that Z never finds Patrice. Cruelty, or kindness? I guess that will be up to the viewer.

It is a story of how lonely we all are and how letting the beauty of a city, slowly discovered, into ourselves can sometimes fix that problem.

I lean against the door frame, exhausted now that my project is complete. I am so happy with it, I almost don't care about what grade Monsieur Deschamps gives me. I know that I've done good work here — and I could not have done it without Serena.

Who is probably at the Eiffel Tower by now. I wonder if she's taking selfies with that human carton of milk I saw her flirting with on the bridge earlier today. Is she gushing about how relieved she is to be in Paris with another tourist and talking about the crazy French guy she was stuck with for most of today?

Of course, she'd be right to call me crazy. I was the one who made a scene at Maison d'angle, forcing us to leave the place, because my ex-girlfriend worked there and I assumed that she'd still be so into me, *she* would make a scene.

Everyone moves on, eventually. And if I got the whole

situation with Martine *that* wrong, what else am I totally wrong about?

I flop down on the same chaise longue where Serena flopped down almost twelve hours ago. Her suitcase seems to glare at me from its spot beside the door to Olivier's room. She will have to come back here at some point, and I will have to face her. I start rehearsing what I might say, but beyond an apology — that I'm not even sure she'll accept — I have no idea what that will be.

I don't know how interested Serena will be in my explanation — partly plagiarized from Martine — that I have realized I tend to run away when someone gets within reach of my emotions. That, because I'm so used to people leaving me — either by choice, like my father, or not by choice, like my grandpapa — I test their patience, to put them in a position where they prove that they *want* to be around me.

From the chaise longue, I can still see the photos hanging on the lines. The first one, the beginning of the sequence, is the first photo I took of Serena today, when she was sitting in the exact spot that I am now, with her head in her guidebook, her lips pursed as she tried not to cry in front of a stranger. Now I see how alone she must have felt, in a foreign country, without the family she was supposed to be sharing it with.

I'm alone, too, Serena. Not that I want to be.

"I'm sorry, I'm sorry, I don't speak *any* French, and I feel so terrible about that!"

The voice is muffled, because it's traveling up from the lobby, but I can tell it's American. Then I hear Thierry telling someone they can't go any farther. I'm off the chaise longue and across the room in seconds, pulling the door open and hurrying halfway down the stairs.

The view of the lobby spills out in front of me, almost like Serena is being painted into my vision. She's standing where she was when I saw her for the first time this morning, pointing to the stairs, as if to tell Thierry that she wants to go up.

She wants to see me.

Thierry looks at me. "Is she with you?" he asks.

I nod, and I have to bite the inside of my cheeks to keep from smiling, and remind myself that it's entirely possible Serena has come back only for her suitcase, so that she can take it to the American guy's hotel.

We go up to the dorm without saying a word. Inside, I gesture toward her suitcase and open my mouth, when I see her head turning in the direction of my room. Once again, I am crossing the living room in seconds, to stand in the doorway — blocking her view.

"What is that?" she asks.

We are standing so close together that, when she looks up at me, I can see that her eyes are red. She's been crying. "It's not what you think …" I tell her.

She says nothing. And I can't very well pretend that she hasn't just seen a room full of photos … of her. So I stand aside.

She walks into my room, looking at each photo in the sequence. She gets halfway along, to a shot of her in the Louvre, frowning at her phone, at a photo *she* took of the *Mona Lisa*. Turns and gawks at me. Starts to say something but seems unable to find the words for a second. Finally, she gestures vaguely at the whole display.

"What is all this?"

"My project. It's … It's you … if that is okay?"

She doesn't answer. She just turns back to the photos.

"It's not as weird as it looks," I tell her, talking fast, trying to reassure her before she storms out. "It was only as I was printing the photos that I realized, the story was *you*. This is how I can capture the city, through your eyes. Obviously, you are not taking the photographs, but I see something so open and vulnerable in your expression — pure emotions — that I can see the effect that Paris has on you … and that tells me more about my city than even the most perfect shot of the Eiffel Tower or whatever."

I really wish I ended that better. But my mouth outpaced my brain, and I ran out of points to make.

Serena says nothing. She's just moving from photo to photo, looking at each one for a few seconds. I prepare myself to get out of her way, deciding that I won't try to stop her storming off or defend myself if she starts yelling at me.

"Jean-Luc …" *Here it comes.* "This is … amazing. I honestly don't think I've ever seen photos of me where I look so *like* me. Does that make sense?"

It kind of does, kind of doesn't, so I nod and shrug at the same time. Change the subject, before it can get any more awkward. "How was the Eiffel Tower?"

She turns away from me, checking out the next photo. "I didn't make it up there."

I hate to admit it, but my pulse quickens a little when I hear that she didn't share that meaningful moment with someone else. "Why not?"

"It just" — she pauses for what feels like a long time — "didn't feel right, once I was there."

Now she turns around, facing me but keeping her eyes on the carpet. "Because, the moment I was about to check off the main point on my list for the Romance Tour, I suddenly stopped feeling romantic. Recreating my parents' trip, walking in their footsteps was …" Her mouth tightens, and she shakes her head at the floor. "It just wasn't right. Even though I was at the tower with a guy who seems like he was designed especially for me, I wasn't feeling the excitement that I know my parents felt when they were together. Oh, man, I don't know how I'm going to make this up to Ethan …"

"You should not have felt like you had to go through with the date," I tell her, "just to spare a boy's feelings. His feelings are not more important than yours."

Now she looks at me. "I know that. But I do still feel a little bad, because Ethan's not a bad guy."

"I am sure he is not."

"And you're kind of an asshole sometimes."

Now it's me who's looking at the floor. I can't exactly argue with her right now.

"But you know what?" she goes on. "When I get home and tell my dormmate about my trip to Paris, when I want to remember the joy of being here, it's going to be you I talk about. The Louvre, Shakespeare and Company, getting on the wrong damned boat … Even all the bickering we did." I dare to look up, see her gesturing again to the Serena shrine I'm suddenly less self-conscious about. "Every part of this trip that helped me not only remember my dad but also … taught me some things about myself."

"Like what?" I ask, surprised that my voice doesn't tremble.

"That I won't be able to connect with anyone if I don't feel able to be myself with people. But in a weird way, seeing myself through someone else's eyes showed me who I really am."

"Someone amazing." It's out before I can ask myself if it's a good idea to say that, if it's too cheesy.

But she just smiles, lets her eyes fall to the floor for a moment, then looks back up at me so suddenly, I flinch. "I hope you're not so French that you'll laugh if I get all sincere and American on you for a minute."

"I am half-American, don't forget."

"I didn't. I, um … Wow, this is strangely difficult. I want to thank you."

I can't think of a single thing that she should thank *me* for. "But I ruined your trip."

"Yeah, you did. But it needed to be ruined. If you hadn't been so allergic to sticking to a schedule, if you hadn't been so irritating — if you hadn't been *you* — I'd probably have gone on the Romance Tour, crossed off everything on my list, taken a few photos home to Mom and Lara … and gone back to being the girl sleepwalking through her life, feeling only sadness, all the time. Thanks to you, I realized it's okay to forget *some* things, sometimes."

I keep quiet. Anything I say now is going to ruin the moment. But we end up staring at each other so long that we both start grinning — both of us a little confused, a little shy and a little excited.

"So ..." I take one step toward her and stop. I suddenly don't trust my legs to keep me upright. "You didn't see any of the light shows tonight?"

She laughs and shakes her head. "I got right up to the elevator, then turned around."

"Then we should go," I tell her. "If we leave now, we should be able to catch one of the last shows. From the Trocadéro, the view will be amazing. Especially now the fog is lifting." I hold out my hand to her. "Come on."

She doesn't move. "It's really okay, Jean-Luc. I'm done trying to create 'moments' in Paris. Mom doesn't need my scrapbook, so I don't need to get a photo of the tower anymore."

I keep my hand held out and close the distance between us. Take her hand in mine. It feels kind of cold, because she's been outside, but when she squeezes my hand, a fire runs through me.

"Not for a photo," I tell her. "Let me show you Paris."

She looks at me for a long moment, her eyes shining as they flit from side to side. "Sure," she says. "That sounds great."

I squeeze her hand back, and we walk out of my room together. Just as I have my coat on and am about to leave the dorm, Serena stops.

"Almost forgot something ..." she mumbles, fumbling in her cross-body bag and taking out her crumpled, wrecked itinerary. She leaves it on top of her suitcase, then walks back over to me and takes my hand again.

We head back out to the city together, charting our own course.

CHAPTER FIFTEEN

SERENA

9:58 P.M.

Jean Luc and I are running hand in hand along the Fountain of Warsaw, in the Gardens of Trocadéro, moving so fast I cringe, worrying that the wine bottles he's carrying in a plastic bag in his other hand — which cost him fifteen euros from the store near his dorm — might get smashed.

The long rectangular basin we run along is lit by bright lights, and the water explodes with arcing jets. A fine mist is falling over us, but I don't care. I'm too exhilarated. Of all the things I expected to happen during the Romance Tour, running through Paris at night with a French boy was not on the list. But that is what's now happening, and I'm definitely not complaining about it.

I laugh and tell Jean-Luc to be careful as we weave our way through the tourists, who are standing stock-still and staring behind us, waiting for the Eiffel Tower to do its thing at ten o'clock. That's what we're here for, but — to be honest — it's basically an afterthought.

We reach the end of the path, and I continue toward the stone steps that lead up to Musée de l'Homme. Jean-Luc pulls me to the side.

"What are you doing?" I yelp. "We're going to miss the show."

"Over here," he says, guiding me to the top of the basin, just behind a series of idle water cannons that look like they're aimed at the Eiffel Tower. Unlike the paths lining the basin on either side, there's hardly any people down here. Probably because the glow of the streetlamps can barely make it this far.

I guess my doubts are obvious, because Jean-Luc grins at me. "It's more peaceful. Less tourists!"

"Hey! *I'm* a tourist," I protest, following him anyway. From here, there is no one to block our view — we can see the tower from top to bottom. Right now, it's lit up in the red, white and blue of the French tricolor.

Jean-Luc puts the plastic bag down and takes out one of the wine bottles. Thankfully, it's not broken or cracked. "*Merde!* I have no corkscrew."

I drop to one knee, starting to untie my shoelaces.

"I know I made faces at those sneakers," he says, "but this is not the time to throw them away!"

"Just watch," I tell him, slipping the shoe off and taking the wine bottle. I use my fingernail to tear off the label, then stand the bottle in the shoe. "I should be able to pop the cork out …"

"By doing what?" Jean-Luc asks. "Beating it on the ground?"

"That's right."

"That will never work!"

I make a face at him. "Clearly you don't go down any YouTube rabbit holes on Friday nights." Then I lift the shoe-bottle and slam the sole — and the base of the bottle — down on the ground. Jean-Luc flinches like one of those water cannons made a sudden noise.

"You are going to ruin your sneakers," he mumbles. "Actually, keep going!"

It takes longer than I've seen it take online. My shoulder starts to ache after a while — but soon, the cork has edged out enough that we can pop it all the way.

"Don't ever doubt me again," I say playfully, offering the bottle. Jean-Luc waves it away, gesturing that I should go first. "*Merci.*" I take a sip, thinking that I sure have taken advantage of the lower drinking age in Europe today.

When I hand the bottle to him, his whole body is bathed in dark blue. The light show is beginning. And it's beautiful, especially the way that the tower seems to be radiating the colors, which swoop over us in slow, almost comforting waves before turning into reds and greens, broken by white stars. It's pretty amazing, but not enough to keep my attention off just how close Jean-Luc is standing to me, how his hand is brushing against mine again, as if he's suddenly nervous about taking it. And I'm nervous, too, which is ridiculous because we basically held hands all the way here.

But that was us being practical, making sure we didn't lose each other in the Parisian Christmas crowds. This is … *different*. Now, as the lights from the tower become suddenly muted, the gasps of appreciation around us fading to a murmur, I feel uncertain all over again. This is a big moment, potentially a perfect end to a story I might be telling for a while, once I'm back home. It'd be really great if I didn't ruin it.

I move my hand toward his, to let him know it's okay. I'm kind of blushing, too — it is all kind of ridiculous but in a nice way.

He takes my hand, threading his fingers through mine. My fingers are stiff from the cold, and I fumble when trying to interlace my hand with his, and we end up with a kind of mangled grip on each other.

That I am not going to fix. Because it might not be a perfect fit, but it feels good. It feels like how *we* hold hands.

And now I'm staring at the French boy I've known for less than a day, his face lit up in the vivid colors the Eiffel Tower is painting Paris with. He's looking back at me, and it's like I'm seeing him for the first time.

He was a stranger this morning, but through him, I got to see this city and find my own version of it — not simply relive my parents' trip. I found a way to both keep Dad in my heart *and* take a first step in moving on from my grief.

I can't believe that, just a few hours ago, I was wishing for a concussion that would knock the memories of this "sucky" Paris trip right out of my head. Right now, I don't want to forget a single thing that happened today.

Jean-Luc turns to face me fully, and I feel my hand tighten around his. Is he going to kiss me?

But that's not what he does. Instead, he asks a question. "How did you know Ethan wasn't right?"

The answer comes to me so quickly, I barely have to think about it. "I just did. I mean, it's not like Ethan's a bad guy or anything. He's a great guy, actually. But he ... he didn't *see* me. You know?"

Jean-Luc's dark eyes reflect the light show, flaring green and red. His face stays so still, I wonder for a second if he doesn't like my answer. But then he nods. "I know what you mean. It is only today that I realized, I could never really *see* Martine. I mean, see her as in, really understand her. Perhaps that is because I was not meant to ... It was not the right thing ..."

He pulls our intertwined hands toward himself, holding mine against his chest. "The right thing is when you both see each other."

I close the gap between us so quickly, I barely think about how unlike me it is. Jean-Luc gently takes my shoulder with his free hand and pulls me in closer.

We kiss.

We don't see any more of the ten o'clock light show.

✳

11:30 P.M.

As fun as it was to drink red wine straight from the bottle at the Trocadéro, I much prefer drinking from the glasses in Jean-Luc's dorm.

Jean-Luc's sitting on the floor, his head resting on my shins. We're holding hands lightly. I'm starting to feel a little sleepy. I hope the bed in Olivier's room is comfortable.

"When do you need to catch your train to London?" he asks me.

"It leaves at two," I say. "So I guess I have to be at Gare du Nord for one o'clock, right?"

"Then we should make the most of the morning," he says, through a yawn. "That doesn't leave me much time to take you around, so that you can see *my* Paris."

"What makes it 'your' Paris?"

From the way he looks into his wineglass, I can tell he's a little shy. "You know … my neighborhood, the places that I know."

"That sounds interesting. I gotta say, I'm curious to see where this" — I gesture to him like he's some kind of exhibit in a gallery — "came from."

My momentary prickle of fear that artistic French guys won't react well when gently mocked is soothed when he just smiles at me. "It will be a Paris without itineraries, without scrapbooks."

I sit forward and kiss the top of his head. Lean back and look into his eyes.

"And no cameras?" I ask.

He smiles up at me. "No cameras," he agrees. "We will walk, and we will just … *see*."

"I'd like that," I tell him.

We kiss again. And again.

SERENA

SIX MONTHS LATER

"You're not seriously going to make me watch *Doctor Who*, are you?" Anthony sounds legit worried.

Charlotte just laughs at him. "No, of course not. Although, it will be a very easy way to get my sisters to like you." It's first thing on a Thursday morning in June, so the observation deck of the Empire State Building is pretty deserted. Just beside me on my left, Charlotte and her boyfriend hold hands and stare out toward the East River, but I get the feeling that Anthony is really looking out toward England. He and Charlotte are catching a red-eye tonight, although Anthony was almost going to bail until his older brother agreed to look after their dog, Mistake. It kind of blows my mind that those two got a dog *the day they met*. But what really blew my mind was when Anthony and I once shared Brooklyn stories and found out that we went to the same high school (he was ahead of me by one year). Even more freaky was figuring out that his older brother, Luke the Cop, was the same Luke the Cop that Lara dated in her freshman year of college. I chose not to tell Anthony how much like a puppy dog Luke was when he was around Lara, just in case Anthony idolizes his big brother!

"Those two are funny," Jean-Luc murmurs, putting his arm around me. I don't think he's let go of me since he turned up at the dorm this morning, having first spent the weekend with his dad. Absence might make the heart grow fonder — Skype and FaceTime make it grow very, very needy!

"I can't believe you dragged me up here again," Anthony mumbles, as he and Charlotte walk off along the deck. Jean-Luc and I walk in the other direction, coming to face the Hudson River on the opposite side.

And just like Anthony seemed to be looking at London, Jean-Luc is very definitely looking at New Jersey.

I take his hand and can tell from how tense it is that something's on his mind. I know what.

"How was it?" I ask him. "Seeing your dad?"

He doesn't take his eyes off the view. "Awkward at first ... and often. And my two stepbrothers are kind of annoying. But they're good kids, really — and my father is maybe not the bad guy I thought he was. You know, back in April, he offered to fly out to Paris for the funeral." Jean-Luc's grandfather passed away in the spring. "He and Mama talked for a long time. I think it was good for both of them — they can forget the past now."

"So your mom's okay with you spending the summer here?"

He nods. "She wants me to have a relationship with my dad,

with my stepbrothers." Then he smiles awkwardly, his shoulders bunching up around his ears. "Also, I think she has a new boyfriend. She met him in one of her art classes. So she's probably happy I am out of the country."

"Oh, she introduced you to Michel, finally?"

He turns to look at me. "How do *you* know about Michel?"

"Oh, please, your mom emails me every week. Sometimes, we even Skype."

Jean-Luc just laughs, shaking his head as he looks back out to the Hudson. "Looking after Grandpapa for as long as she did must have been very tough on her."

I squeeze his hand, pull him to me a little. "You still miss him?"

I see his jaw clench as the breath catches in his throat, his eyes closing briefly as he wills himself not to cry. "I do," he whispers. "I think I probably always will — just like you'll always miss your papa. It might never go away. But that doesn't mean you can't appreciate the present, right?"

I pull him in for a soft kiss, then rest my head against his chest, feeling completely at ease. I don't know how long this feeling will last, but I hope it's a long time. Especially now that Jean-Luc will be coming here in September, on a study-abroad year at NYU. I'm trying not to get *too* excited about that.

After a few more moments gazing out over the Hudson, I take both his hands and start leading him toward the exit. "We should go get breakfast," I say. "If you're going to go apartment hunting this afternoon, you'll need all the energy you can get."

He's resisting, and I'm about to turn around and tell him to *hustle, damn it*, when I see that he's grinning at me.

"What's with the look?" I ask him.

"Nothing," he says. "I just like looking at you, that's all."

I smile and shake my head. "Okay. As long as you *see* me, too."

ACKNOWLEDGMENTS

Huge thanks again to all the people who read so many itera-
tions of this story: Samantha Noonan, Charles Nettleton, Clare
Hutton and Kate Egan. A hat-tip to all the creative bravehearts at
Working Partners, who support and inspire on a daily basis; and
to Alexandra Devlin and our friends at Rights People, for helping
us send these figurative kisses all around the world!

Follow Catherine Rider on Twitter @CRiderYA.

JAMES NOBLE is an editor who also writes under a variety of pseudonyms. He was born and raised in London. He went to primary and secondary school in London. He went to college in London. He got his first — and only, and current — publishing job in London. He has intermediate Cockney rhyming slang, loves pie and mash (though he recoils at the mere mention of jellied eels), and never forgets to "mind the gap." But he still loses far too much of far too many days daydreaming about what it'd be like to live in New York.

Eternal gratitude to my parents, Debbie and Jimmy, and to my brothers, John and Joe (and Emma!), for putting up with me in all the ways that you do! Much love to the Brennan-Finnegan and Bailey/Cheshire Clans, who I'm proud to call my family. A "mad" hat tip to all the supportive writers I know. Thanks, most of all, to my friend and collaborator Stephanie, whose daily example never leaves any choice but to always be better.

STEPHANIE ELLIOTT is a book editor who moved to New York immediately after college. She has never been mugged, ridden a Citi Bike or been harassed by a rogue Elmo in Times Square (though one did get a little salty with her, once). She feels strongly that bialys are better than bagels, yellow cabs are better than Ubers and pizza must NEVER be eaten with a fork. She loves visiting London, where people are SO polite! She lives in Brooklyn with her husband and five-year-old daughter.

Love and thanks to my parents, my supportive friends, the Elliotts, the Lanes and the indescribable city of Paris, which always inspires me. Particularly big hugs to Dan and Maggie, my two loves who are always up for exploring with me. And a special thanks to James, for his love of this story and his amazing contributions!

WHAT ARE YOU READING NEXT?

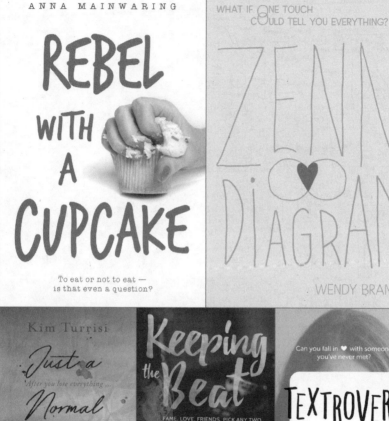

MORE GREAT BOOKS

ALSO AVAILABLE

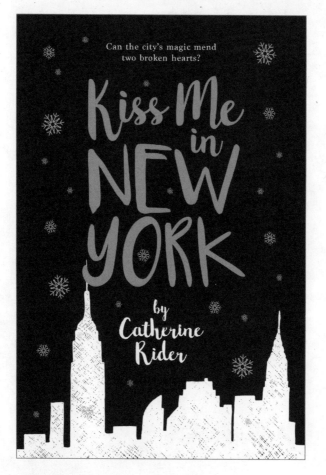

"Sweet and satisfying."
— *Publishers Weekly*